The Wreck and Rise
of Whitson Mariner

Books by S. D. Smith

Publication Order:

The Green Ember

The Black Star of Kingston (The Tales of Old Natalia Book I)

Ember Falls: The Green Ember Book II

The Last Archer: A Green Ember Story

Ember Rising: The Green Ember Book III

The Wreck and Rise of Whitson Mariner (The Tales of Old Natalia Book II)

The First Fowler: A Green Ember Story

Ember's End: The Green Ember Book IV

Best read in publication order, but in general, simply be sure to begin with The Green Ember.

The WRECK & RISE of Whitson Mariner

S. D. SMITH

ILLUSTRATED BY ZACH FRANZEN

Story Warren Books
www.storywarren.com

Trade Paperback edition ISBN: 978-0-9996553-6-8
Also available in eBook and Audiobook.

Story Warren Books
www.storywarren.com

Cover and interior illustrations by Zach Franzen.
www.zachfranzen.com
Map created by Will Smith and Zach Franzen.

Printed in the United States of America
20 21 22 23 24   02 03 04 05 06

Story Warren Books
www.storywarren.com

For Norah Claire

Laetare ergo iuvenis in adulescentia tua et in
bono sit cor tuum in diebus iuventutis tuae
et ambula in viis cordis tui et in intuitu
oculorum tuorum et scito quod pro
omnibus his adducet te Deus
in iudicium.

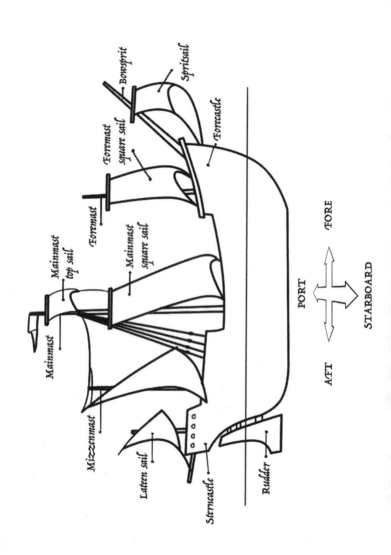

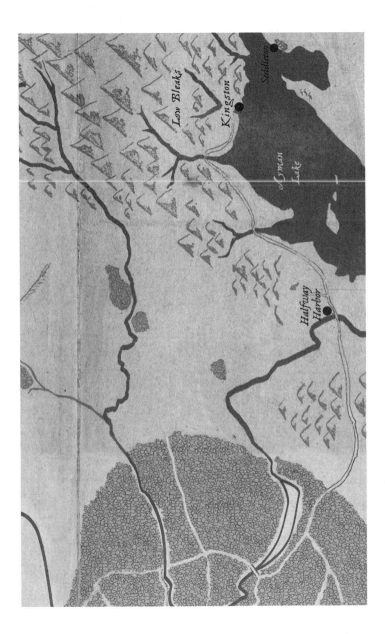

Did it burn? Yes, and still it burns. I loved the royal family, and I was there when they were torn apart. I couldn't sit by and watch, so I followed them into the fire.

From the Journal of Massie Burnson
King's Officer

Tales of Old Natalia

Chapter One

King Whitson Mariner received his lords and captains in *Vanguard*'s large cabin, along with a few more guests. It was crowded and warm for the gathered rabbits, but the food was good, the mood high, and Queen Lillie was a magnificent hostess.

Whitson gazed across the table at Lillie, who bravely engaged the most boorish lord at the table in conversation. She had done it all evening, kindly including the most reluctant and rude while seeing that the least assertive were also given attention. In the lumpy, ill-formed blob of dough that was this meal, she was the rolling pin, smoothing all and helping it become something of worth. Whitson marveled at his wife.

Lillie looked so lovely this evening and fairly glowed in the flickering lamplight. She glanced across and caught his eye for the merest moment, her head inclined ever so slightly to his left. Following her subtle direction, he saw Brindle Cove, sitting with his head down, nervously folding and unfolding his hands. Red-furred Brindle was the son of a poor farmer and planned to follow his father's calling. But during the voyage from Golden Coast he had taken to the sea at once. Recently, because of his excellent seamanship, he had been promoted to the rank of lieutenant. Brindle had never been at such a function and clearly felt woefully out of place. The wide-eyed rabbit seemed ready to dart out of the room at any moment.

"Lieutenant Cove," Whitson said cheerfully, "a glass with you, sir?"

"Uh, um." Brindle Cove looked up, stuttering. Recovering himself, he bowed his head. "Your Majesty is very kind." He raised his glass, and they drank together.

"May I congratulate you again on your promotion, Lieutenant?" King Whitson said, leaning closer. "And if you and your parents would do me the honor, I would be grateful if you would be my guests for dinner in our cabin tomorrow night."

"Your Majesty," Cove said, his mouth falling open. "It would be our great pleasure."

"You would honor me, sir," Whitson said, smiling. Then he whispered confidentially to the young lieutenant, "It will be less stuffy than this." Cove breathed a sigh of relief. He bowed his head respectfully, then raised it to show a bright smile and shining eyes. Whitson turned to the other side of the table. "Captain Suttfin, sir. The bottle stands by you." Captain Suttfin smiled and poured a glass, while Whitson stole a grateful glance at Lillie.

"If only Captain Suttfin dominated the seas as skillfully as he dominates the bottle," Captain Grimble said. "He's a better sipper than a skipper."

Several bucks in Grimble's corner laughed. Captain Grimble's father, Lord Grimble, leaned against the wall, appraising the room with narrowed eyes.

Whitson frowned. He had been afraid of this. Before he could interject, Captain Suttfin answered. "Skill alone is no measure of virtue."

"No, indeed," Captain Grimble replied. "But

there are no fortunes to be made by playing well with others and having the best manners."

"If there were, you'd be a pauper, Grimble," Commander Tagg said.

"He's the best captain here," Commander Usher called, casting a sideways glance at King Whitson, "and no one can argue with that. He'd out-sail and out-fight any rabbit alive."

"Surely we'll make our fortunes together—sail on together, fight together—serving our king," Captain Walters said, looking into Captain Grimble's haughty face. "Will we not?"

Grimble smirked but said nothing. An agonizing silence followed as Whitson searched for the right words to calm this brewing storm.

"I will serve the king . . . a drink"—Lillie swept into the center of the room—"and one for you as well, Captain Grimble," she added, handing a glass to each buck. A third glass appeared, which she took, extending it to-ward the corner of the room. "Lord Grimble, will you not have a drink with the king and your son?"

"My son . . . the king? Only," the old lord said, walking forward with a knowing smile, "if the queen will join us."

"I would be delighted to join you," Lillie said.

"To a true queen," Captain Grimble said, raising his glass before Whitson could, as was his proper place, raise a toast of his own. "May her beauty be the light by which a new and distinct kingdom dawns."

"To the beautiful queen," Lord Grimble said, with a wry smile at his son, "and a new kingdom."

Whitson's anger rose, but before he could speak, Lillie took his arm and led him away. They passed Lord Grant, who had been close enough to see the encounter. Lord Grant glared at Lord Grimble.

"Where are we going?" Whitson whispered, arm stiff as they moved to the other side of the room.

"A tactical retreat, for now," Lillie whispered back, smiling. "We'll fight on other fronts, my love."

"I suppose I should thank you," Whitson said.

"I am always with you, husband," she answered, locking eyes with him.

"I know it, Lillie. What would I ever do without you?"

She fixed the chain around his neck from which swung a ruby gem and smiled up at him. "Wreck and ruin?" she whispered back.

"Most likely so," he said, glancing around. "Lillie, when can I end this, do you think? If we cut it off before there's a fight, we'll call that a major diplomatic victory."

"Probably an hour or so, my dear," she said. "But now would be a good time to toast them all."

He nodded, and they turned to face their guests. "Friends," Whitson called, quieting the lively table, "may I propose a toast?"

"Hear him!" Lord Grant called, looking straight at Lord Grimble. "Hear our one true king!"

The king nodded to the noble old rabbit and put his arm around Lillie. "All of us stuck together during the passage from Golden Coast, through the Battle of Ayman Lake, and through the wintering we've just endured at Halfway Harbor. For that, I salute you." Many of the guests began to tip back their glasses, but the king went on. "Now, shipmates, we set off on what I hope is the final stage of our journey."

"Hear, hear!" Captain Walters called.

"May it be," Lieutenant Cove said brightly.

"So, gentlerabbits all, let us drink," Whitson said, raising his glass high, "to our journey—the journey to our unknown home."

They drank together, clapped, and cheered the king. On the deck above them the deckhands cheerfully danced and sang. Though Lillie had worked her magic and the evening was a plain success, the Grimbles still brooded near the edge of the room. But even they joined in when the gathered rabbits sang.

"We have sailed over endless seas,
That have somehow now come to an end.
And we, having settled at home,
Have decided to sail out again.
Oh, what has got into our minds,
That we give up the life we had?
It only can be that we've caught the disease,
Of the seas and we've all gone mad!

So, hie, and so, hey, we're sailing away,
On the tide, with a bride like a dream!
In her bosom we fly, under glorious skies,
We are wed to the ship of the seas.
We are bred for the ship of the seas.
We'll be dead on this ship of the seas.
What ya' said on this ship of the seas?
Said, 'We'll be dead, on the ship of the seas!'"

They sang on and on and had many more toasts before Whitson bade them farewell.

"My friends, I do not like to be the one to say it, but here is where we part. Captain Grimble and Commander Usher return to *Burnley*, and Captain Suttfin and Commander Baghurst to *Steadfast*. We are three ships, but one community. May our three vessels carry us safely on our passage home."

"Thank you, Your Majesty," Suttfin said, bowing low.

Captain Grimble, uneasy for a moment, stepped forward and bowed slightly without making eye contact. "Safe travels, sir."

"Captain Walters, please see that our guests have everything they need," Whitson said.

"Aye, sir," Walters answered, crossing to confer with his fellow captains. "Lieutenant Massie," he called, "please step on deck and alert the boat crews that their captains will be leaving soon."

"Aye, sir," Massie said. With a neat bow, he turned and left the cabin.

Lillie came alongside Whitson, sliding her arm into his. "My king, you did it."

"My queen," he replied, gazing at Captain Grimble's foul expression, "what have I done?"

"I have a feeling …" Lillie began brightly, but then she winced, and finally she sighed.

"Me too," Whitson replied. "A very, very bad one."

Tales of Old Natalia

Chapter Two

On deck, Lieutenant Massie Burnson weaved through rings of dancing hands and ducked beneath spars and sails. Musicians played while deckhands and passengers danced, clapped, and laughed beneath the rising moon. He found Jimmi Docker slumped over a barrel beneath the bowsprit.

"Jimmi," Massie said, nudging the lanky rabbit. "Hey, wake up. It's time to row your captain back across."

"I ain't not ar'sleepin', Buckrod," Jimmi snapped. He sniffed indignantly as he got slowly to his feet.

"You could have fooled me," Massie said, hiding a smile behind his hand.

21

"It ain't not a bit hard to fool a feller what's got such a pea brain as you, Massie Burnson." Jimmi rubbed at his eyes while his one free ear, which poked through the single hole in his head wrap, rose slowly like a battered flag hoisted aloft on the mainmast. But the old rabbit's ear seemed to get stuck halfway up, bending at its end.

"No offense taken," Massie replied, smirking.

"I beg ya ta' reconsider it, and upon farther examinification, please do take it for offense," Jimmi said, reaching in the right pocket of his bright striped trousers for his pipe. "And when you've got it in yer hands, stick it in yer pipe," he continued, shoving his pipe in his mouth. "And smoke it up!" he shouted through clenched teeth.

"I'm really sorry to have woken you!"

"As I said, Massie Burnson, I were not even a little bit ar'sleep. Anyway, what's your name all about? Burnson? Was yer pap a fire?"

"No, his name was simply—"

"Nobody cares, Buckleburp," Jimmi shouted, stuffing his pipe into his left pants pocket, "what your bloomin' name might be and just how flammable yer pap was!"

"You clearly needed more sleep," Massie said.

"I weren't ar'sleep!" Jimmi bellowed.

"My, my, you're testy today, Jimmi," Massie said, raising his hands. "Seriously, my friend. What's wrong?"

"Only . . . well," Jimmi began, eyes flitting from his hands to Massie. "It's only, well . . . only that you woke me up!" he bawled. Then he hurried off to gather his boat crew.

Massie laughed as he watched Jimmi, oar in hand, collar *Steadfast's* crew, dragging them away from dances and other delights.

Captain Grimble appeared on deck, his perpetual scowl deepening. Jimmi, dragging Frill Able away from a very sweet doe named Ginny, accidentally bumped into Grimble.

"How dare you!" Captain Grimble cried, cuffing Jimmi as the docker bent to pick up the oar he'd dropped.

"Beg pardon, Captain Duke, sir," Jimmi said, raising the oar. "I were only a'gatherin' Cap Suttfin's boat crew from their revels. I didn't not mean no harm to your lordly magnificence."

The music had stopped, and everyone on deck watched. Massie frowned. Captain Grimble whipped out his sword and sent it slicing through

Jimmi's oar so that the stunned docker was left holding two stubs. Grimble extended the blade toward Jimmi's neck. "If there were any order in this place, fools like you would be marooned and left for dead. The weak element needs weeding out."

Jimmi gulped as Captain Grimble, scowling at the watching crowd, sheathed his sword quickly and stomped off toward his own boat crew. Commander Usher followed, sneering at Jimmi and Frill.

Massie breathed a sigh of relief. In a few minutes the king came on deck, and a merrier spirit renewed. The music resumed, and the last dancers lingered.

When all the captains had boarded their boats and their crews were slowly rowing them back toward their ships, Massie stood on deck alongside the king. Prince Lander appeared at Whitson's side and received an embrace from his father. The black star patch on the prince's shoulder matched Massie's own, though the red stains on the white border around Prince Lander's star were unique.

On a chain around his neck, the young prince wore the Green Ember. It was the center stone of the crown he would one day inherit from his father, with all the burdens that involved. The king's Ruling Stone was also on display this night, the ruby medallion that signified his right to the throne. The Ruling Stone and the Green Ember were usually tucked under shirts and worn discreetly. But on this full-dress occasion, they were worn openly, side by side now, red and green on royal father and son. They matched the red and green double-diamond standard that flew high atop the mainmast above.

"Lieutenant Massie," Lander said, smiling as he saluted.

"Your Highness." Massie bowed. "How'd you sleep?"

"Not too bad," Lander began, wincing a little. "To be honest, Lieutenant"—he glanced back at his father—"I've been having bad dreams."

"I'm sorry, sir," Massie replied, kneeling beside the prince. "I've had a few myself over the years. Can I help?"

"They're always about being carried off," Lander said, eyes worried. "Either it's me and I'm taken far away, or I'm just watching while them I love are taken. Carried off. I'm just sitting there, powerless."

"You're not powerless, sir," Massie said. "You're a good sailor and a brave fighter."

"It's true, son," the king added. "Your masters say you're getting quite good with your blade."

"Beg your pardon, sir," Lander said, "but having skill and being brave aren't the same."

"That's true," Massie said, gazing into the prince's eyes. "But I see the bravery there inside you. And when it leaps out, it'll be good you have skill to guide it."

Prince Lander had grown so much in the last year, and not only in stature. Massie was loyal, of course, and would do anything to serve and protect the royal family. But he also liked the prince and was proud of how the lad had responded to the calamity that had nearly ended their community on the shores of Ayman Lake.

The Battle of Ayman Lake had not been won. No, there had been far too much loss to call it a victory, but Captain Fleck Blackstar had ensured that neither was it completely lost. Captain Blackstar had saved King Whitson and dealt a blow to their monstrous enemies. In a desperate last-minute act, he had used blastpowder barrels to blow up their overrun ship, killing many of the raptors and finally driving them away. In the hurried council that followed, the king decided to divide the community and make Fleck Blackstar a lord. Lord Blackstar was charged with staying behind at Kingston, operating the coal mine and building a war burrow. The Kingston rabbits had a specific charge, to be prepared to fight the ruthless raptors who had stolen so many souls from the ships of Whitson's company and the streets of Seddleton. No one knew what had become of those taken. Seddleton had been destroyed, and so many innocents had lost their lives.

Now the king's company would sail on in three ships, newly built or repaired, up the river to what they hoped would be a new home. They had reason to be hopeful, but Massie feared that they had not left all their enemies behind.

Massie rose and gazed out at the Grimbles' boat carrying the curt old lord and his son, Captain Grimble, back to *Burnley*.

Whitson caught Massie frowning and nodded. "Your thoughts, Lieutenant?"

Massie looked down. "I don't like to say, Your Majesty."

"You think it was a mistake to appoint Grimble as captain? It's all right; please speak freely."

"Well, sir, I understand what you mean to do by the appointment, and I admire you for it. But I'm worried, yes. Not just about what's ahead but about the past several months when he was scouting the river."

Lander frowned and looked up at his father.

"I wanted to get him out of Halfway Harbor," Whitson said. "He would have torn the community apart and gotten into all kinds of mischief here."

"It worries me, Your Majesty," Massie said, "what mischief he got up to while he was away."

"I know Grimble's a gamble, Massie," Whitson said, nodding. "But I've got to unify this community."

"I hope it pays off, Your Majesty," Massie said, doing his best to smile.

"What happens if we lose the gamble, Father?" Prince Lander asked. "Do the monsters come back and carry us off?"

"I hope," the king said, squinting into the distance, "that we never have to find out."

Tales of Old Natalia

Chapter Three

Soon after their departure from Halfway Harbor, the river grew narrow and their soundings found a far more shallow depth. *Burnley* was sent ahead, since she knew the way, and *Vanguard* tracked behind her. *Steadfast* had stayed on an extra day to complete the final stages of leaving their winter home at Halfway Harbor. King Whitson ordered watches set from each ship's prow to scout the river for danger, in addition to the regular officers of the watch and the sailors in their ordinary rhythms of rotation. Massie, keen-eyed and expert with a bow, kept a regular vigil in *Vanguard*'s prow.

* * *

"How am I going to die?" Prince Lander asked. "Will I be carried off by those monsters?"

"I don't know, Your Highness," Massie said. "But it's better to live as you will want to have lived rather than spend your time worrying about the end. You are right here in your story. Don't skip ahead." Massie stood alongside the young prince on the prow of *Vanguard*, scouting the increasingly turbulent river for perils.

"Lieutenant Massie, would you call me 'shipmate' and not 'Your Highness'? After all, we're in the same company," Prince Lander said, pointing to the black star patch on his shoulder.

"We are shipmates, sure. But you're also my prince. I'm afraid I can't pretend you're not. You must be a prince, and I must be your loyal servant."

"I suppose so," the young prince said, frowning.

"What's troubling you? Have you had those dreams again?"

"Of being carried off?" Lander sighed. "Yes. I'm always afraid something bad will happen."

"I'm sorry to hear that, sir. Though it was some time ago, the memory of Seddleton is still fresh," Massie said, peering into the distance with a scowl. "Now I'm growing afraid myself—afraid of this poor visibility. I can't see well enough in this growing fog."

"I can still see *Burnley*'s mast there, two—no, three!—points off the starboard bow. She still has her sails set," Lander said. "She should hail if there's danger, should she not?"

"Aye, but Captain Grimble doesn't always hail us with great haste. Please pass the word for Captain Walters. Say that I beg he will take in sail. Say we cannot see well enough to scout."

"Aye, sir!" Lander said, and he scurried off.

Massie kept at his vigil as fog swept over the ship. He could see almost nothing now, and he turned back to peer through the gathering mist on deck. The ship was not yet slowing.

"On deck there!" he shouted at a passing sailor. "Hayes! Go and wake the king."

"The king?" Hayes asked.

"Aye, the king," Massie said. He swerved through coiled ropes and sailors at their stations. "Captain Walters?" he called. The deck was dense with fog. There was no response. "Commander Tagg!" No answer.

He found the bell rope and rang it hard. "All hands, take in sail! Heave to and drop anchor. Where's the officer of the watch? Find Captain Walters and Commander Tagg!" He heard calls and answers, the sounds of sailors stumbling through the fog.

King Whitson appeared on deck in his nightshirt, rubbing at his eyes. Just then a rending crack sounded, and the ship ground to a halt, spilling all hands forward. Pained groans and harried cries accompanied the grinding churn of wood pressing against rock.

* * *

"Boathooks!" Whitson called above the clamor. He rose slowly, with a wince, from the deck. "Deploy boathooks and get us off that rock! Master Owen, take a lamp and check the hold. I have no doubt we are sprung. Start the pumps."

"Aye, sir!"

"Hamp!" Whitson shouted to a hurrying sailor.

"Aye, Your Majesty?"

"Please go below and beg the queen to come on deck."

"Aye, sir!"

"Carry on, bucks!" the king shouted above the buzzing din on deck. "We must save our ship! Remember what precious cargo we carry."

"It's too late, Your Majesty!" Massie shouted, panting as he ran up. "I've been over the side. *Vanguard* is wrecked. It's only a matter of time—"

Before he could finish explaining, the ship lurched and began sinking rapidly.

"Where is *Burnley*?" Whitson asked. "Can anyone see her sails?"

"There's no sign of her, sir," Massie said. "And

they don't answer hails."

"They never warned us, neither," Prince Lander said, joining his father.

"Launch all boats," Whitson called. "Start the mothers and children over first, then every doe. Massie, you go. Lead them to shore."

"Aye, sir," Massie said, then he hurried through the press of active sailors. "Make a lane! All boats overboard!"

Hamp reappeared, looking nervous.

"What is it, Hamp?" the king asked.

"It's the queen, Your Majesty," he said, swallowing hard. "Queen Lillie is gone."

"Gone?" Whitson asked. "Gone where?"

"By Flint's own sword," Lander said, eyes wide and terrified. "She's carried off."

Tales of Old Natalia

Chapter Four

Massie pushed through the dense press of rabbits at the portside rail, leapt onto a battered barrel, and shouted, "All hands!" The panicked rabbits turned their frightened eyes on him as the wind picked up, sweeping away the fog. Fresh rain sprayed the deck. "Orderly, now, shipmates. Let the boats be lowered and the does and younglings be carried across to shore." The ship lurched lower, unbalancing everyone. Massie grasped a stray rope, righting himself on the settling barrel. "Quickly, now!" he cried, and, gripping the taut, twisted halyard, he swung across to repeat his orders on the starboard side.

Glancing aft as the driving rain replaced the fog, he saw that something wasn't right on the command deck. But he had his orders. The boats came down, inelegantly handled, to splash in the swift river. Ropes held the small boats to the sinking *Vanguard*, while sailors set about their harried evacuation in the swelling storm.

Massie joined in, handing down one after another of the waiting rabbits to strong-armed sailors in the boats. When a boat was full, the crews pulled with all their might for the shore. Once there, they set their soaked passengers on the bank. Then, gripping their oars, they shot across the river to reload and do it all again.

Vanguard continued to slip, the water rising ever higher as the creaking vessel seemed certain to come apart at any moment. Massie handed down a bawling baby to her mother's waiting arms and, the boat being full, called out the order to row. Turning back to stage the next boat's passengers, he saw only a scattered band of mostly elderly rabbits, among them Mother Saramack, a widow and a councilor or at King Whitson's assembly.

"Mother Saramack," Massie called, motioning her over to the rail. "If you please, ma'am! The next boat will take you over."

"When the rest are gone," she said, gripping the rail, and her elderly companions nodded.

Massie frowned and turned back to the rail, where King Whitson stood with Prince Lander. "Take him across yourself, Massie!" the king said, pushing the prince toward him.

"Your Majesty, you must take him! I'll see to the rest here."

"It's not a request, Lieutenant," Whitson called. "I'm looking for Lillie! Listen to me, Massie. No matter what happens, to me, or to this ship, do not leave my son!"

"Aye, sir!" Massie called, clasping the prince as the surging storm whipped the sails overhead. The king, sword in hand, disappeared below-decks.

Massie fought to keep from going after the king and turned his attention to the young prince. Prince Lander gazed after his father, his eyes haunted. The boat returned, rowed by its weary crew, and Massie nodded for the prince to leap down. "Now, sir, if you please!" Reluctantly, Lander obeyed.

A rough grinding sound turned into a rending crack, and the ship began to tear apart on the rock.

Massie felt the deck give way, saw the rending split of the prow ahead. After one woeful glance back, he turned and leapt for the boat.

Tales of Old Natalia

Chapter Five

Massie snagged the outstretched arm of a strong sailor, who helped drag him into the boat. "Row for the shore!" Massie cried as *Vanguard* broke apart around them. Prince Lander stood and stared back at the sinking remnants of the big ship, scanning the wreck for any sign of his parents.

"We'll find them," Massie said, urging the prince to sit. "Aft now, bucks!" he cried to the boat crew. They obeyed, deftly rowing through a cascading avalanche of *Vanguard*'s shattered remains, finally emerging behind the wreck, where they could more safely make for the shore. Though his eyes eagerly scanned the wreckage, Massie saw nothing that gave him hope.

The boat ran aground on the pebbly shore, and the crew leapt out. Several bucks offered the prince a hand, but he sprang out and waded to shore, eyes darting back across the water.

Massie felt torn. He wanted to take the boat out at once and try to find the king, but he had promised to stay with the prince. With the queen also missing, there was a good chance Prince Lander was the last royal alive.

Massie glanced around the bank. Rain-soaked rabbits huddled in silence, staring in disbelief as pieces of *Vanguard* floated down the river. Beyond the wreck, Massie saw white sails carrying *Burnley* farther away. He seethed.

They knew all along. They set us up for that wreck. The Grimbles betrayed us all. He sank to his knees, bitter bile rising in his throat.

"There!" a nearby rabbit shouted, pointing upstream. "The king's in trouble!"

Massie followed the frenzied cries to the point upstream where several stout sailors were plunging desperately into the water. He leapt up and ran along the bank, anger at the Grimbles for their obvious treachery and fear for what had become of the king and queen propelling him on. He heard cries all around him. When he reached the gathered crowd, he pushed ahead. That's when he remembered Lander.

He swiveled back, scanning the shore for the young prince. Panic swelled as he searched every section of the visible shore. He could not see the young buck anywhere. Turning back, he ran for the point where they had disembarked together.

"Prince Lander!" he cried. "Has anyone seen the prince?"

Most were so occupied with other urgent matters that for many precious seconds he could find no one who had noticed the prince. Then a shivering young doe called to him. "Lieutenant Massie, sir," she said, pointing to the woods. "He ran that way."

Massie nodded and, with one agonizing glance back at the commotion on shore, sprinted for the tree line.

He sped past a frightened huddle of rabbits, many very young and all vulnerable. He hated to dash off in the midst of such awful need, but his promise to the king rose like a beacon in his mind, and he ran on.

Massie made for a small gap between two

large trees and plunged into the dense forest.
Eyes darting, he found a broken branch ahead
and hurried that way. "Prince Lander!" he called,
breathing hard. "Come back!" He sprinted on,
ducking branches and occasionally catching sight
of rabbit tracks in muddy breaks in the brush. He
didn't stop to examine the tracks, but something
didn't seem quite right.

He ran into a dense thicket that slowed him
down a moment, and he fought through bushes
and brambles until he emerged into an open space.
The clearing was a rough circle, with a solitary tree

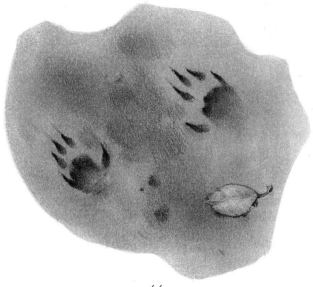

standing in its midst. Prince Lander was bending beneath the old oak.

"Your Highness!" Massie shouted, jogging up. "What were you thinking?"

"Shhh!" Lander said, turning his wide eyes toward Massie and raising a finger to his lips. The rain fell hard, and puddles pooled around the oak.

Massie frowned and stepped closer. "Why did you run off? There are terrible things happening back on shore. How could you leave like that?"

"I heard my mother scream," he said quietly. "And I followed."

Massie's eyes grew wide, and he knelt next to the prince. "Which way?"

The prince pointed across the drenched clearing. Then he pointed down. Massie bent to examine the ground. There, in the mud, were several sets of tracks. A few were rabbits, he could easily tell. But there were other tracks as well, wide and heavy, with thin, sharp toes. Massie had never seen anything like them.

"Monsters?" Prince Lander asked.

Massie squinted at the prints. "Maybe so."

Lander stood up and took a deep breath. "Let's go," he said.

Massie glanced back the way he had just come and winced at what he was leaving behind. Then he nodded, and they jogged through the last of the soggy clearing and ducked into the brush.

Tales of Old Natalia

Chapter Six

Whitson descended into the bowels of the ship, and he searched everywhere he could find a measure of air. Lillie was nowhere to be seen. He cast away his sword and waded into the large cabin. He took a deep breath and dove down, hunting in the flood for his beloved. He could see very little, but he hung on as long as he could, peering into every corner. When he at last came up for air, he saw that the ship had sunk lower and the flood had risen higher. With a surge of water, the small pocket of air disappeared. He snatched a breath and dove again, desperately trying to reach the hatchway. But he heard a groaning crack and watched as the wall gave way and the ship began to break up.

He was trapped. Underwater.

Whitson tried to rise but was beaten back by a rush of water. Wood parted, and he was propelled forward, smacked and tossed by surging debris. He flailed in vain against the crashing torrent. He had very little air left and felt his panic begin to fade into an inescapable oblivion.

He was mere moments from the end.

Then Whitson found a foothold on a sliding blastpowder barrel and used it to propel himself upward, all the while being pulled sideways in the undeniable current. He gained a few precious feet and kicked hard for relief. But as he shot to the top of the cabin, he hit the unyielding roof, still in place and blocking his escape.

Terror gave way fully to acceptance, and he closed his eyes with pictures of Lillie and Lander in his mind.

There was another booming tear, oddly sonorous in the water, and the ship tore apart. With a sudden gushing jet, Whitson shot through the broken deck to the surface, only just sliding past the front edge of the jutting rock on which his ship had wrecked.

He gulped in precious air, coming awake in the

rush and roar of the splintering wreckage. Whitson reached for the rock, trying to find a handhold on anything that would arrest his perilous advance.

He missed.

With a cry, he was pulled by a sudden certain tug of the deadly current. He felt a hand—a strong hand—grip his wrist. He looked up past wet red fur and into the eyes of Brindle Cove.

"I've got you, sir," Cove shouted.

Whitson could say nothing, only cling to his rescuer and allow himself to be pulled onto the large rock. He rolled over and coughed—coughed as he never had, spewing water and gasping for breath. When he finally was able to rise to his knees, he looked around and found a few other survivors like him on the woeful rock.

"Lieutenant Cove," Whitson wheezed, "am I right to assume you have saved more than myself today?"

The other rabbits nodded while Cove helped the king slowly to his feet. "We've done our best, Your Majesty," he said. "The boats are coming to fetch you over, sir."

"Thank you, Lieutenant," Whitson said, gripping the young buck's arm. He looked to the riverbank, where a band of eager bucks was crowding. A boat emerged, rowed by strong sailors and commanded by Captain Walters.

Whitson looked back upriver, then turned and squinted through the pelting rain at the white sails disappearing in the distance.

"We are betrayed," Whitson said bitterly. "They have broken faith with us and left the most vulnerable members of our community to die."

"Aye, sir," Cove agreed, his jaw tight. "And they have broken their oath to their king. What will we do now, Your Majesty?"

"We'll make shelters here and wait for *Steadfast* to come up. Then we'll see to them," he said, pointing to *Burnley*'s distant sails.

"*Burnley*, sir?" Cove asked. "But they have a vast crew of fighting bucks, and we're in no shape—"

"She is no longer to be called *Burnley*, Lieutenant Cove," Whitson interrupted. "She doesn't deserve that good name. She is now *Desolation*."

Tales of Old Natalia

Chapter Seven

Massie was pleased with how well Prince Lander kept up in this rain-soaked chase to rescue the queen. They dodged through thickets and dashed around trees, always following the elusive tracks of the queen's captors. Queen Lillie must have been taken right off the ship in the moments before Captain Grimble led them into a disastrous trap. Massie did not know how it was possible. Now *Vanguard* was destroyed, and the families and most vulnerable members of the community—those Whitson had insisted on carrying on his own ship—were marooned on the shore behind them. Massie did not know if the king had even made it to shore. What was happening back there? Had Mother Saramack and the other widows survived?

He fought down a welling dread.

Part of him thought it best to turn around and take the prince back to the relative safety of the shore. But the queen had been taken, and there was no one else to help her. Not in time, at least. He had to follow on and do what he could to free her. An angry part of his heart was eager to meet her captors. Massie's hand went to his sword hilt. He glanced back at the young prince and saw he did the same. But was Lander ready for a fight?

The two rabbits ran on in the slackening storm, the young prince trailing Massie into ever-thicker forest. Massie kept up a challenging pace, his eyes flitting quickly between the way ahead, the tracks below, and the prince behind.

Is that movement in the distant thicket to the right? His keen eyes were so eager to see something, he was afraid he might only be imagining it. He hurried forward, now trying to scan all around as he led the prince ahead. A few minutes later, he thought he saw a splash of black in the trees above. Was it only the dark bark or a fleeting shadow? *Do shadows move?* Massie frowned.

"You've seen the ghost too?" Prince Lander

asked, edging near Massie as they slowed to pick their way through a tangled patch of thorny brush.

"The ghost, Your Highness?"

"Something's out there," Lander said, "and it's hard to spot."

"Don't give in to fearful fancy. It's probably nothing."

"I'm not as experienced as you are, Lieutenant Massie," Lander said, "but in my short life I've found it's almost never *nothing*. It's something. Monsters are real; I know that. Ghosts probably are too."

"Just be ready with that sword, sir," Massie said. "I'd wager our steel will find more than mist if this *ghost* attacks."

"I'm ready. Whoever took my mother will answer for it."

Massie nodded. The two emerged through the tangled thicket, and their path was clear for a few minutes. They neither saw nor heard anything unusual. They hurried on.

Massie ducked a dangling limb and emerged into another small clearing, then slowed to examine tracks and allow the prince to catch up. He paused over a troubling set of footprints, again trying to determine what might have made such a mark. The prince drew near, breathing hard.

"Are you all right, Your Highness?"

"I'm . . . completely . . . fine," Lander managed to say between gasps.

Massie smiled. "What do you make of these tracks? Our ghost?"

Lander, still breathing hard, bent to examine the strange shapes. "It looks like a monster, but not the monsters we've seen."

"Not the monsters we've seen," Massie mused, his brow wrinkled. "If there's anything worse than the monsters you know—" he began.

"It's them you don't," Lander finished.

"Are you scared?" Massie asked.

"Yes," Lander admitted, "but I remember what Captain Blackstar said to me. That we have to keep loving what's on the other side of this fight—the other side of this rescue—and that will have to make us brave."

"He is the best of rabbits."

"Aye," Lander said, tenderly touching the black star patch on his shoulder, "he is. I wish we had him with us."

"As do I," Massie agreed. "But he's far away in

Kingston, and we must do all we can with what we have."

"Yes, sir."

Fearing that this conversation was draining away the prince's resolve, Massie gripped the young prince's shoulder. "Are you angry?"

Prince Lander nodded, his jaw tightening.

"I understand, Your Highness. That's good. But we must keep in control. When we find them, we need to be cautious. I need you to do just as I—"

Before Massie could finish, they heard a loud rustling in the brush just ahead. Prince Lander, eyes wide, broke for the spot in a dead sprint, ripping his sword free as he ran.

"Wait!" Massie shouted, charging after the prince. "No!"

Lander hit the edge of the clearing just as Massie had nearly caught him, and they both plunged in, one after the other. Massie's heart raced as he broke into the brush, dodging a large tree as he reached out to collar the charging prince. Just as he snagged the young rabbit, he heard a loud snap and felt his feet being swept up, followed by his entire body, as he and the prince were caught up and bundled together.

They were hanging, upside down, in a net. The prince had triggered the trap's catch, and now they hung there, helpless. Their swords, knocked away in the jarring jerk, lay useless on the ground.

"I'm sorry," Prince Lander said, his voice thick with panic. "I'm so sorry."

"I'm here, Your Highness," Massie said.

Massie struggled to free a hand. *If I can only reach my knife.*

Then they heard a noise.

Footsteps. Close. Closer.

"Oh no," the prince whined. Massie heard the footsteps, felt the new presence, but could see nothing but an upside-down forest through a web of braided cords.

Massie could not reach his knife. He was pinned and helpless. Behind him, the footsteps stopped. He heard the unmistakable sound of a sword being drawn.

Tales of Old Natalia

Chapter Eight

Ring Whitson stepped from the boat onto the stony shore. Everywhere he looked, he saw disaster. Hurting, terrified rabbits of every age huddled in small groups, trying to get dry, tending to wounds. Some sat wide-eyed, shaking their heads in disbelief. Others hurried from group to group, panicked faces begging for news of missing loved ones. *After all we have been through from outside dangers*, Whitson thought, *to be thus betrayed by those in our own community. The Grimbles. What a wicked treason this is.*

He had been told of the almost certain fate of those left on the ship when it came apart and others murdered when Lillie was taken, including brave Commander Tagg.

The widows had been on board at the end. He was devastated. He felt Mother Saramack's loss keenly. She had become more than a valued and loyal member of his council. She was like a mother to him. She was irreplaceable. They all were. All the lives surely lost grieved and enraged Whitson. The cargo—some of it more precious than he could calculate—was lost as well. He thought of the inheritance crate and its priceless relics within. Sacred charges from the old king, Fay's book and Flint's stone sword among them. The Ruling Stone was also gone. This was a betrayal that did more than abandon and kill; it cut off connections to who they were as a community. It unmade their history.

Lord Grant appeared, his face saying all Whitson needed to know. But the king asked anyway. "No sign of them?"

"No, Your Majesty," Lord Grant answered gravely. Queen Lillie was his daughter, and the young prince, his only grandson. "But Lieutenant Massie is missing as well. I've sent word around for anyone who saw Lillie, Lander, or Massie to come to me."

"Thank you," Whitson whispered. He dropped

to his knees, his hands covering his face. "This is my fault. I shouldn't have trusted Grimble."

"You never trusted Grimble," Lord Grant said. "You only gave him more credit than to be capable of something so incredibly wicked. None of us would have believed this was possible."

"It's still my fault."

"It may be," Lord Grant said, bending to whisper in the king's ear. "But you cannot mourn and moan right now, Your Majesty. We need a leader."

Whitson stood up and glanced around at the gathered rabbits. Most were looking at him with worried expressions. He wiped his eyes. "You're right, of course. I have to make this right again. I have to . . . to somehow get to Captain Grimble and answer this treachery. I have to face him."

Lord Grant's head tilted; then the noble old lord looked down.

Whitson glanced around. He saw several officers nearby. "Captain Walters."

"Aye, Your Majesty?" the young captain answered, jogging over.

"Gather all my officers and lords," Whitson said, "anyone not doing essential work. Go now."

"Aye, sir!" Walters said and then hurried to the nearest band of officers to relay the king's orders.

"What will you do?" Lord Grant asked.

"My best for them," he said, nodding at the bands of survivors scattered along the shore. "And for them. . ." he said, turning to point the way Captain Grimble and *Desolation* had sailed, "my worst."

* * *

Massie had never felt so helpless. He hung upside down in a rope net, pressed against the prince he had been charged to protect. And he could do nothing. Nothing at all.

The haunting presence behind them was still. Massie had heard the sword being drawn and could faintly make out steady breathing, but all else was silence. The rain had stopped.

"You can do with me what you want," Massie said, his voice even. "But leave the lad."

He heard a snort.

"He's just a child, and of no importance," Massie went on. "If you let him go, I'll do whatever you ask, surrender any treasure, give any service. I will be your slave."

A guttural laugh sounded, and they heard footsteps. Close. Closer.

Then a strange face appeared, upside down, in front of Massie. There were eyes, but the face was a strange tangle of what looked like looping reeds, one tan, another brown, in a disturbing pattern that arrested Massie. White around his eyes, the creature had a mouth set with large, hard teeth. Prince Lander stole a glance and cried out, "The ghost!"

Massie was frantically trying to make sense of the image when he spoke. The voice was deep and hard, full of gravel and somewhat garbled. "A ghost?" he said, and then he laughed again. "You may call me that. And this is my island. I have haunted this place for many months. And you are trespassing."

"We'll leave," Massie said. "Just let us go, and we'll leave."

"You won't leave, I think," the ghost said, moving out of sight again, "until you have done what you came to do."

"Yes," Massie said, straining to see. "After that."

"They have your queen, it seems," the ghost said roughly.

"How do you know that?" Massie asked, struggling to free himself, without any success. "Are you part of it?"

"I see everything here in my hauntings," the ghost replied. "And though I've done evil in my

day, I'm no taker of souls."

Massie struggled desperately to free himself once more. "Let him go!" he cried.

"Young Massie Burnson," the ghost said, appearing before him again. "Settle yourself down, lad."

"How do you know my name?" Massie asked. "Who are you?"

"Why," the ghost asked, "don't you recognize me?" He reached up furry hands and lifted off the elaborate mask he was wearing. Massie's eyes grew wide.

"Galt?" he asked, barely believing what, or rather who, he saw.

Tales of Old Natalia

Chapter Nine

Aye, Massie lad," Galt said. "It's me."

"But I thought you were dead," Massie said, eyes wide.

"And I, you," Galt answered, raising his sword.

"Galt, no!" Massie shouted as Galt brought down his sword, slicing through the top of the rope net. The two prisoners fell to the ground, landing hard. Lander groaned, but neither he nor Massie was able to stretch out or stand. The net still held them tight.

"I don't want to kill you," Galt said, "but neither do I want you to kill me. Can we agree on that?"

"Of course," Massie answered. "Just get us out of this net."

"I'm afraid it's not that easy," Galt said. "I'm a traitor by your laws. Your duty is to capture me and turn me over for justice, is it not?"

Massie looked away.

"In fact," Galt continued, "you and I both know how any judge of your company would sentence me. For I," he said, looking away, "betrayed the king. I left him, left all of you, at the moment of crisis on Ayman Lake. I ran away when Fleck begged me to help the king. I know what sentence I'd get."

"You're right, Galt," Massie said. "It would be our duty to do just as you have said. But right now, we don't have time for any of that. You know yourself that the queen's been taken. We have to find her."

"Then we are at an impasse. If I help you, I condemn myself."

"If you help us," Lander said, finding his voice, "you might redeem yourself."

"Your Highness?"

"It's possible that my father is dead. If he is, I am the only person who can pardon you. If you can help us find Mother, I will pardon you, or beg my father—if he is alive—to do the same. But whether or not I can save your skin, cut us free so we can help the queen."

Galt stepped back, then turned and gazed into the forest. Then he turned back, nodded, and worked at the top of the net, unbinding the cinched top so that the net fell limply to the dirt. The two rabbits stood slowly and stretched.

"Your Highness," Galt said, "while I consider myself a free rabbit, bound to no authority but my own will, I am grateful for your assurance."

Lander nodded.

"I know you'll have questions," Galt said, "and I will do my best to answer them. But answer one question for me."

Massie nodded.

"Is Fleck alive?" Galt winced as he asked.

"Lord Blackstar is alive," Prince Lander said. "He is head of the community at Kingston."

"Lord Blackstar?" Galt mused, looking at the prince, his eyes filling with tears. "I was just getting used to him as a captain. Now he's a lord."

"He saved us all," Lander said.

"I'm no great believer in making one buck higher than another," Galt said, "but if one was to be elevated, it should be him. The noblest rabbit

67

I ever knew."

"The queen, Galt. What do you know?" Massie asked. "Please tell us as quickly as you can."

Galt sat down and motioned for them to do the same. Reluctantly, Massie sat on a stump, while Lander, face intent, began to pace. It was clear he would not sit.

"I came to this place after I left Fleck and fled inland during the battle at Ayman Lake. I trekked many miles along the river for what felt like endless weeks. I made a raft and drifted, finally finding this island. On that first night here, I decided to go no farther. I was wracked with regret and despair, and, exhausted and starving, I ate the yellow berries on the east bank. I fell into a fevered dream from which I thought I'd never wake. In the dream I saw myself traveling on, southwest, and finding a community of wild rabbits."

"What of the queen, Galt?" Massie interrupted.

"I come to that," he answered. "I awoke the next morning with a new purpose. I found good food, drank from a clear stream in a valley at the heart of the island, and built a shelter near the stream and its pristine pool. I made a little garden and began to grow healthy again, driven on by a lingering vision of a journey southwest.

"All was well for many weeks, until one night, as I lay in my poolside hovel, I awoke to the sound of strange music. Or it was like music, only it was unlike anything I'd ever heard: a dark, lisping, wet, whispering kind of song. Beneath a high, haunting melody came a rumbling chant that chilled me. I gathered what I could and fled up into the hills, abandoning my shack. But driven by a mad curiosity I returned and sat to watch the valley from a high black crag covered in brush. I lay on the stone and watched, afraid but certain I could not be seen."

Lander had stopped pacing now, and his eyes bore into Galt, as if weighing the older buck in a balance.

"I tell you the truth, Your Highness," Galt said, getting to his feet. "I stared into the moonlit valley and waited for the singing strangers to appear. Then they came, black-robed and hooded, carrying torches. They surrounded the pool and sang on, their eerie chants rumbling like tide-breakers. They performed some dark rites that culminated in them bringing a raft into the middle of the pool. On it lay squirming some small living thing.

I could not make it out in the moonlight, but dread fell on my heart, and my breath caught. They disrobed and waded into the water, great scaly brutes with fat legs, long tails, and split flicking tongues. With a grim chorus of wet roars, they fell on the raft in a frenzy. I turned and ran, desperate to get away. I ran and ran and ended up far away, frightened like I'd never been before."

"And it's these monsters who have my mother?" Lander asked, clenching his fists.

"Aye, Your Highness," Galt answered, "or will soon. I believe it was rabbits who took the queen, perhaps with one of the dragons. But they will bring her to the valley pool."

Massie felt his stomach twist as he glanced up at the sun. "Grimble?"

Galt nodded. "I have haunted these woods since that night by the pool and have seen many

70

amazing things in my ghosting. Grimble had friends on your ship, and they, with some help, have carried off the queen."

"Help?" Lander asked. "From the monsters?"

"Aye, sir," Galt said, shaking his head. "Lord Grimble has allied with dragons."

Tales of Old Natalia

Chapter Ten

Will they never come?" Whitson sighed as he gazed up the bank toward the lookout he had posted. "Come on, Captain Suttfin. Where are you?" He heard his officers hovering nearby, discussing what occupied his own thoughts.

"How long might *Steadfast* take to arrive?" Lieutenant Cove quietly asked Captain Walters. Both stood a discreet distance from King Whitson as he continued to pace up and down the shore, shooting longing looks upriver.

"It might be as much as a day on," Walters whispered back. "Captain Suttfin's a good sailor and the ship is quick, but only at her fastest could she be anywhere near here."

"And the fog and rain have no doubt—"

"Exactly," Walters said.

A shout rang out from the upriver watch, and Whitson charged up the shoreline.

"What was the hail?" Walters asked, rushing to catch up to the king.

"I couldn't make it out, Captain," Lieutenant Cove called, "but the king's away!"

Whitson spied the small knot of rabbits and slowed slightly when he saw they had their swords drawn and were facing the forest, their backs to him. A few of them held bows at the ready. Walters and Cove ripped free their own blades and surged forward. "If we may, Your Majesty," Walters said, not waiting for permission. They jogged ahead until they reached the small band of wary rabbits, who were all gathered around a tree, in which sat a strange creature. The tree bore deep gashes.

"What is this?" Whitson asked, eyeing the strange tangle of braids and big eyes of the half-obscured creature in the tree. Then confusion gave way to urgent anger and he shouted, "Do you know where the queen is? Have you seen my son?" He blinked away the tears starting in his eyes and focused on the form. The creature was silent, only moving his head back and forth in slow rotations.

"Shoot him down," Whitson said, nodding to an archer.

"Wait," the creature said, his voice a gruff grumble. Then he extended his fist and let fall a glittering green gem, which snapped taut and swung from the end of a gold chain. The creature held it out, letting it swing. *The Green Ember.* Whitson gasped as the creature went on. "This is a token I bear as a symbol of the trust the giver has placed in me," he said, voice coarse and menacing. "Please send them all away, Your Majesty. I would like to speak with you alone."

Walters made to speak, some objection no doubt, but the king raised his hand.

"Leave us," he said. "Watchers, return to the rock and resume the lookout for *Steadfast*. Walters and Cove, back to the camp, and see that all is prepared."

"Your Majesty?" Lieutenant Cove asked, wincing.

"Follow your orders, Lieutenant," Whitson growled. Then, more gently, "It will be all right."

"Aye, sir," Cove said, backing away with the greatest reluctance as he eyed the creature in the tree.

When they were alone, the creature swung down and landed in front of the king. He reached out the emerald gem and laid it in the king's open hand. Then he took off his elaborate mask. "Your Majesty," Galt said, "I bring you word from Massie and your son."

"Is he all right?" Whitson asked, for now less concerned with where this once lost rabbit had come from.

"He is, Your Majesty," Galt said, "and so, I think, is the queen."

Whitson's wet eyes widened, and he managed to ask, "Both? Unharmed?"

Galt nodded, but his eyes were grave. "For now."

Tales of Old Natalia

Chapter Eleven

Massie pushed on through the thickening brush, the prince following hard after him.

"Will Galt keep his promise?" Prince Lander asked. "Will he really go to Father at the shore and warn them?"

"I don't know, Your Highness," Massie answered, slicing at a ragged root that wound around a thorny patch of brambles. "I believe he will. We must believe, for everything depends upon it." His stroke broke the tangle, and the green and brown threads unraveled to open a path deeper inland. "My sword grows dull with all this hacking, but if Galt is right, we should be getting close."

"Use mine, Lieutenant," Lander said, extending the hilt of his bright blade. Massie nodded, and they traded swords. With a deep breath, he sent the fresher sword into action, cutting a stubborn path toward the center of the island. By Galt's advice they had avoided the easier way and were working inland through an untouched section of forest, thick and nearly impenetrable.

"If Galt told us true," Massie said, glancing up through the scattered spray of light above, "we should find a break in this soon and get into the rim of the valley."

And they did. Picking carefully through the last of the thicket, they skirted a clearing and, following Galt's instruction, circled around to a cluster of black rock. Massie crept through the last yards of the soft forest floor, and his foot found hard, dark stone. The prince inched in behind him, and they stepped carefully through the thin alley leading to the tree-covered cliff that had been described to them. From here Galt had seen the dragons at their horrific rites, had heard the sickening song and chant they raised. Massie, crawling on his belly, reached the sheltered lip of the black crag. He gazed down into the valley. He saw the pool in the clearing, the small shack, and a fire swirling smoke into the afternoon air.

Massie nodded back to the prince, who scurried up beside him.

"Do you see her?" Lander asked, whispering.

"I don't," Massie answered, "but I'd wager she's being kept in that shack." He pointed to Galt's crude shelter, not far from the pool.

"Agreed. What's your plan, Lieutenant?"

Massie looked into Prince Lander's eyes, once again gauging the young rabbit's nerve. "You will have to fight, Your Highness. Are you ready for such work?"

"I am prepared to do whatever I must for my mother," he said. His eyes glistened, but his jaw was set.

"Good. Remember that they left the most vulnerable members of our community, the babies, mothers, and the aged, to die. Remember, my prince, that they are monsters all. Even the rabbits."

"Especially the rabbits," Lander growled.

Massie nodded. Then a splash brought their attention back to the valley pool, and turning their heads, they peered below. Massie's stomach churned at the sight.

A black dragon, large, strong and shiny, his split tongue flicking in and out, waded into the pool. He reached out a scaly clawed hand to pluck flotsam from the water. Troubling the water as little as possible, he made his slow way out, his head bowed until he reached the bank. There he added the flotsam, a collection of leaves and branches, to a large pile. Then he took a handful from the other side of the pile, the dry side, and tossed it into the fire.

Massie's eyes thinned into slits. He looked at the prince.

"I know what to do."

Tales of Old Natalia

Chapter Twelve

Steadfast, at last!" the lookout called. Whitson's head swiveled around, and Galt rose from where he had been sitting.

"Walters, there!" Whitson shouted.

"Aye, Your Majesty?" Walters called back.

"Captain, I beg you will bring *Steadfast* in, update her on our situation, and proceed with our plan."

"Aye, sir," Walters called, and he hurried toward the mooring.

"Galt," Whitson said, turning back to the conference, "I have no time. If what you say is true—" He hesitated a moment.

"I assure you it is, sir," Galt said, filling the silence. "I have no love for the dragons and their horrible rites." He looked at the deep gashes in the tree, made by dragon claws. "I wouldn't ever deceive Your Majesty while they scheme to take our young ones, and"—he looked down—"well, I have told you what they plan. It's despicable how Lord Grimble has agreed to it. But I've heard it with my own ears."

"We have been bargained away to buy them safety and a kingdom that the Grimbles can set up on their own."

"You have, sir. And they ain't likely to do anything but the worst, knowing what they've agreed to. There'll be no honorable surrender if you find them."

"No," Whitson agreed. "We will have to fight them."

"If you can catch them. The north branch is the only way to do that. I'm sorry. The ship makes for the rendezvous on the far side of the island, and if Massie and the young prince fail, the captors will take the queen there to meet the ship."

"Thank you, Galt," Whitson said, his head going down. "You are pardoned of all. That is the past. The future is before you now. I ask you to come along and help us rescue the queen, to somehow deal with the dragons here and with the Grimbles. We need you. And I welcome you back to our community. It may be hard, but rest assured, there is a path for you and a place among us."

"Your Majesty is most kind to say so. But my way lies in the southwest. I have had a vision of a peaceful society built on equality. And I go to find and form it."

"You'll leave us, again?"

"Aye," he said, not meeting the king's eye. "So, farewell."

Galt moved toward the woods, but he stopped beside the tree that bore the long, deep scratches made by the dragons. He put his hands in the marks, feeling their deep furrows. Galt hung his head a moment, then hurried into the forest.

* * *

A few minutes later, Whitson stood on shore with the surviving council members, his lords and officers, and a few others.

"We have been dealt a cruel blow, friends," Whitson began. "We have been betrayed by our own kind. Lord Grimble, Captain Grimble, and every rabbit who took part in the plot to wreck our ship, capture our queen, and destroy our community are under a judgment. The lords have agreed. We are at the edge of our ability to survive. There are new monsters on this island. Dragons. I have it on good authority that Grimble, while he was under my orders to scout ahead and prepare a way for us, made an alliance with these dragons. Lord Grimble has secured a settlement and a tract of land upriver. But he had to promise something."

"What did he promise?" Lord Grant asked, his jaw tight.

"It seems that, years ago, there were wild rabbits living in these parts. The dragons would cultivate these rabbits and use them in their wicked rituals."

"Use them . . . how?" Brindle Cove asked.

Whitson's face twisted in disgust. "For dark rites we can barely imagine," he said. "It seems that Grimble's plan includes separating with his own followers and building a new settlement and, eventually, a kingdom. He has always believed that the old king erred when he appointed me as his successor. Now he will begin again with a new line, his own line, as monarchs in the new world. He has allies in the dragons, if they can be trusted, and us as his currency with them."

"If he means to use us as his way of buying favor with these dragons," Captain Walters asked, "then why has he wrecked us?"

"Because he knows us. He knows we are survivors. He knew we would be decimated by the wreck, gutted by the queen's abduction, and easy prey for the dragons to dominate. He planned to leave us on this island and sail on. He knew that, in no long time, the dragons could make us their slaves."

They were silent then, each face a mixture of grief and gravity.

"Why the queen?"

"I don't know," Whitson said, "but I believe Lord Grimble intends to force her to marry his son and so make the new line more legitimate."

"The queen would never—" Lord Grant began.

"Of course not," Whitson said. "They have underestimated my wife. And they have underestimated us." He looked around, his determined face an anchor for those still adrift in a sea of shock and horror. "We will never let our younglings become food for monsters, be they birds of prey in the High Bleaks or the dark dragons of these parts. We will never rest while the reprehensible treason of the Grimbles and their followers fouls our nostrils."

"But what can we do?" asked Fren Hiddle. She was another old member of the king's council.

"I have come to learn that *Desolation*, formerly *Burnley*, has sailed south around the island and will make for the far side after their ceremony with the dragons. We must be at that rendezvous. I will take *Steadfast* and a skeleton crew, leaving the community to be defended by what forces we have."

"But how?" Captain Walters asked. "How can we catch *Desolation*? She has such a lead."

"We take the north branch of the river, and if we leave at once, we can catch them at the junction on the far side."

"Your Majesty," Captain Suttfin began, but Whitson cut him off.

"We must leave, now," Whitson said, raising his hand.

"Aye," Fren said, her voice thick with conviction. "We'll see to the shore, Your Majesty. Please take every sailor you can."

Whitson smiled at Fren but shook his head. "Captain Walters has made the division. I'll not leave these vulnerable ones unprotected. We sail with a skeleton crew."

"But, sire," Lord Grant protested.

"No, sir," Whitson said firmly. "I have made my decision. Captain Walters," he said calmly, "if you please."

Walters saluted, then turned and began bellowing orders. "All right, shipmates, on board *Steadfast* now, and look lively!"

Whitson longed for the wisdom of Mother Saramack and the other lost widows of his council. His head swam again at what had been lost in the wreck, of both souls and treasure. But mourning, more weeping beside graves and lamenting what was lost, would have to wait. He steeled himself for the task ahead and leapt on board *Steadfast*, his face set hard.

"Weigh anchor!" he cried.

"Weigh anchor," Walters repeated.

Jimmi Docker saluted and, with help from Jake, began to raise the anchor.

"Pull your share, Jake Able," Jimmi scolded as they pulled. "They ourght ta' call ya' Joke Fable, for all the musc-ability you've got!"

"Gah, Jimmi," Jake replied, smirking. "Just

pull harder yourself and do something worthwhile for once in your life."

"Somethin' worthwhile?" Jimmi shot back, his voice high with indignation. "I'm right on the spot when things is thingin', Joke Fable."

"I'd like to see you anywhere near the action when it matters," Jake said, and the nearby hands laughed.

"Just you wait and see, Buckrod," Jimmi said, hands going to his pockets while Jake took all the strain. "I'm there when the gettin's gettin' got!"

Whitson shook his head but said nothing as he and Lord Grant made their way to the ship's bow.

"Why," Lord Grant whispered when they reached the rail, "did Grimble sail south around the island and avoid this shorter northern way?"

"Because," Whitson

whispered hoarsely as he gazed ahead, "this way is full of tricky twists, foaming surf, tide pools, shallow passages, and rocks. Rocks all through."

"Like the one that tore us to shreds?"

"Bigger. And harder to see."

"And it's the only way?"

"It's the only way to Lillie."

Lord Grant nodded gravely. "Then let all be a hopeless hazard, and I will ride through it with you."

Tales of Old Natalia

Chapter Thirteen

Lillie woke slowly, drifting in and out of awareness. At first her head swam, and she could only lie still. The pitch and roll she had grown accustomed to on board *Vanguard* were gone. She knew she was somehow on land.

As her vision cleared, she sat up slowly. Thin wooden walls and some crude stone tools surrounded her mat of woven reeds. A cleverly made stone stool, supported beneath by three stout legs and bound well together to a smooth rock top, was the only furniture in the room. Through a glassless window, she saw a blur of green. Beside the window, there was a closed door.

Where am I?

Then memory of the struggle on board

Vanguard returned. The dark, silent shape in the night. Her smothered scream. The gag and the hood. Strong, scaly hands. The terrible fight as they took her off the ship. On land again. Wrestling her gag free, and her one scream, followed by the blow.

She could feel the pulsing pain from the spot on her head where they had struck her. Lillie tried to rise and move to the door but fell onto the hard-packed dirt floor. She felt the bonds tied tightly around her wrists and legs. She scooted back to the mat and gathered her thoughts.

I've been taken. Who would— But just as the question formed, she knew. *The Grimbles.* She didn't know why, or how, or what would come of it, but she knew the Grimbles were involved. Snatches of their past conversations came back to her in vivid detail, and she began to piece together the probabilities.

They'll find I'm harder to keep than I was to take. Lillie looked around the room, then scooted to where she could grip one of the crude tools in the corner. She began working the dull stone against the rope around her wrists. It was painful to twist to where she could get at it, but it was beginning to work.

The door burst open, and a massive form stood silhouetted in the doorway. A hissing whisper filled the room, and Lillie shivered with a sudden chill. The light behind the creature showed the outline of a claw raised toward her that splayed out like five razor-sharp points of a star. She gasped, dropping the tool. The creature reached down, snagged the tool in his claw, then brought his eyes level with her own.

She could see him now and the scaly armored skin surrounding the lithe muscular form. His forked tongue flitted out in menacing stabs as his eyes narrowed to slits.

"No," he growled. The voice, so slippery and coarse, caused Lillie to shiver again. Tossing the tool out the window, he turned, revealing a strong back that stretched down into a long, powerful tail. As he ducked back through the door, his tail lashed out suddenly, striking the stone stool so hard that it shattered into pieces. Lillie screamed and closed her eyes against the flying shards.

The door closed, and Lillie looked up. She was alone again, shaking on the floor amid the pulverized dust wafting down in the sunlight streaking through the window of the now silent shack.

* * *

Lillie recovered enough to creep to the open window and sneak a glance. A stream flowed down out of the ridge above, forming a clean pool surrounded by smooth rocks. The creature was there, taking dry sticks and leaves from a pile near the pool and burning them in a small fire. The monster's head extended forward, and his back sloped down to his tail. Two strong legs gave him a firm base, and his muscular arms ended in deadly claws. She could see that the creature would be fast and agile, while also possessing bone-crushing strength.

While he burned the dry debris, he seemed to mumble incantations.

Maybe the Grimbles weren't involved. Maybe these lands are teeming with every kind of monster.

Just then a rabbit walked into view in front of the shack. Two rabbits, and then a third. She recognized each of them. They were from Grimble's ship and some of his most loyal thugs. They stayed well away from the dragon as he concluded his burning ritual.

So Grimble is *involved.*

A noise in the forest behind the fire made the monster stop his work and peer around. A second noise of rustling, and the creature motioned for two of the rabbits to follow him into the forest. They ran after the quick creature while the third rabbit, a massive buck called Tarn, remained behind and swiveled to check on the hut. Lillie ducked and remained hidden for a moment. Looking out again, she saw that Tarn was staring ahead at the pool. Another rustling noise sounded in the forest near the hut. Tarn looked from the forest to the fire, to the pool, then again back at the hut. Lillie, anticipating his movements, dodged out of sight once more. When she peeked again, Tarn was gone.

This is my chance. It's probably Whitson coming for me.

She listened carefully, gazing through the open window to see if any of her captors were returning. Then she looked around the room, but there was nothing to slice herself free with. She decided she had to risk it and hope to find a tool outside to cut her bonds in time before they got back. Determined, she took one last glance outside the window.

She barely stifled a scream.

Tales of Old Natalia

Chapter Fourteen

Lillie trembled as she watched her son mount a small raft and float out toward the center of the pool. Lander was covered, except for his head, with what appeared to be a blanket or an oversized cape. She wanted to cry out to him but held her tongue. Lander lay still as death on the raft.

The scaly creature returned from the woods and peered around until he saw the floating form. The monster's eyes widened, and he bared his teeth. His tongue flicked out, and he dashed toward the pool. Lillie's heart pounded as she remembered what that tail could do. It was all she could do to keep herself from screaming a warning. The three rabbits returned as well, with wary glares all around. Tarn resumed his post in front of the hut. They all watched as the beast, now slowly wading into the water, extended his claws toward Lander.

The monster loomed over the prince, reaching down for her only son. Then the young buck's eyes shot open. In one motion he cast off the cape and drove his bright blade into the soft underbelly of the shocked monster.

Lillie cried out then. She dodged sideways and leapt into the door. The door crashed down on Tarn, and the queen rolled outside. The other two rabbits, alarmed at what they had seen in the pool, reacted to the crash and rushed toward Lillie, who was desperately trying to writhe free and get to her son. They closed in on her.

Out of nowhere, Massie Burnson leapt in, landing a devastating kick on the foremost attacker. The stunned rabbit rolled down by the edge of the pool just as Lander emerged to guard him with his bloodstained blade.

"Lie still, or die," Lander growled, eyes wide.

Massie cut Lillie's bonds. He turned to the next of Grimble's thugs, Grenjo, who spun to face him. Massie stepped between Grenjo and the queen, drawing his sword.

"Lieutenant Massie," Grenjo said, laughing as he pulled his own blade free. "Without your bow, you're no match for me. I've trained with Captain Grimble for years, and he's the best sword-wielder alive."

"But I have a club," came a voice from above. Lillie looked up to see another creature, strange in its wild costume and face, drop behind Grenjo and level the unsuspecting buck with a crushing swing to his head.

"Galt!" Massie cried as the club-wielder threw off his mask to reveal a more familiar face. It was a smiling rabbit she barely remembered. Galt. Massie and Galt stood over the rabbit Lander had been covering while the young prince darted to his mother.

"Lander!" she cried, wrapping him in an embrace. "Oh, you were so brave!"

Lander wept and hugged her as Massie used his sword to lift the chin of the third rabbit of Grimble's party.

"Speak, villain!" Massie said, bringing the point of his blade to the buck's neck.

"Your sect is doomed," he answered. "The future is for the brave and the strong. The fighters. The future belongs to the Grimbles."

"You think it's brave to kill the old and the innocent and to ally yourselves with dragons?" Massie asked. Lillie, still squeezing her son, listened keenly.

"There are hard steps up a high hill," he answered, shrugging. "Worth it in the end."

Lillie marched forward, extending a hand toward Galt. "Do we need him, Lieutenant?" she asked Massie.

"Need him, Your Majesty?" Massie asked back, face confused.

Lillie received the club from Galt and brought it around with a crack against the buck, who slumped into a stupor.

"Nice one, Mother," Lander said, his fist clenched.

"Your Majesty," Galt said, bowing quickly. He pointed at Tarn, the rabbit felled by Lillie's door-destroying escape from the hut. "This one is waking up."

Tarn rose slowly to his knees, then glanced around at the dramatically changed scene. His two comrades lay senseless on the ground, and the queen was free. Massie and the prince were there, along with Galt. He shook his head. Lillie stepped toward him, club in hand, as the prince and Massie flanked her. Lillie felt a fury she had never yet known rise inside her, but she breathed deeply.

I must be more than angry. I must be a queen.

"Are there more?" she asked Tarn, handing the club to Galt. She nodded toward the captive. Galt readied the weapon, awaiting her command. "More dragons? More of Grimble's craven back-stabbers?"

"I'm not saying nothing." Tarn smirked. "They'll be back," he said, glancing up at the sun. "Soon, in fact. They'll be here soon. And if I were you, sweet queen, I'd just surrender to me now, so you don't get hurt."

Lillie bristled inside, but all Tarn saw on her face was a cold smile. "Galt, if you please," she said evenly, nodding toward Tarn.

"Wait," Massie said, stepping between Galt and Tarn with his hands up.

"Listen to the wise buck, little doe," Tarn said, a smug grin showing his teeth.

Massie turned back to Tarn, his nose wrinkled in disgust, as he brought his fist forward to meet Tarn's grinning face. The big buck spun down, spluttering. "Your Majesty," Massie said, turning back and bowing to the queen. "Forgive me, but I think we *can* learn something from him that might help."

"Go on, Lieutenant," Lillie said.

Tarn was shaking his head again, hand to his mouth as he checked his many broken teeth.

"How many dragons are there, Tarn?" Massie asked. "How many are coming, and why are they coming here?"

"You broke my jaw," Tarn slurred.

"More than your jaw will break if you don't talk," Lillie said coolly. "Perhaps," she said, glancing back at the pool, "I'll order you tied to the prince's raft and left in the center of their pool."

Tarn looked up, his angry expression giving way to fear. "The pool? Oh no! You killed a dragon! In their sacred pool. Oh no," he said, stammering and trying to get to his feet. "They'll destroy us all. This is a shrine for them. This is where the pact will be formalized. Lord Grimble's coming here. Oh no. Oh no!"

"Listen to me!" Massie said, grabbing the babbling buck by his tunic. "We need to know what's coming. We need to know how to prepare to defend ourselves."

"Or it's onto the raft in the pool," Lillie said.

"There's no preparing for them," Tarn cried, whimpering now. "There's no being ready. They'll slaughter us all. We have to run. We have to run, now!"

"How many?" Massie shouted.

"Twenty, I think? It's not all of them. Most of 'em are away with their king, but this band is enough, believe me!" Tarn said, beginning to cry.

"We have to run. We have to get out of here!"

"Your Majesty," Galt said. "You should go, with the lad. Now."

Lillie nodded. "Where's the king?" she asked him.

"He's running the north branch rapids to catch Captain Grimble out at the junction past the island. He's running a skeleton crew and is outnumbered. Even if he makes it through the rapids, the odds are bad."

Tarn whimpered on, "We *have* to run!" Massie held him tight, raising a fist in warning. Tarn flinched and fell to his knees, weeping.

"Whitson needs help?" Lillie asked.

Galt nodded. "Desperately, ma'am."

"Is there a chance we could—?"

Lillie didn't finish what she started to say. From the trees to their left poured a band of dragons, sniffing the air, tongues darting.

The dragons saw the fouled pool and let loose a bloodcurdling chorus of bellows.

Tales of Old Natalia

Chapter Fifteen

We'll never survive," whispered Jake Able, but his words carried over the silent deck of *Steadfast*. The whispered worries were heard even at the bow, where King Whitson gazed at the rock-strewn rapids ahead.

His eyes never left the swift river. "Take that buck's name," he said evenly.

"Aye, sir," Captain Walters replied, nodding to his steward. The steward scribbled in his book as Jake Able hung his head. His brother, Frill, patted his arm.

"Nice one, Buckrod," Jimmi Docker whispered hoarsely to Jake. "Now he's only gone and wrote your name in his wee book."

"Hamp, there!" Whitson called.

"Aye, Your Majesty!" Hamp replied from the helm, far aft on *Steadfast*'s long deck. Whitson kept his eyes on the rapids ahead, gazing downriver as far as could be seen. He knew Hamp would be nervous.

"Prepare to turn us hard to starboard," Whitson said. He heard a chorus of gasps behind him.

"Starboard, sir?" Hamp asked, his voice breaking.

Whitson expected this. He could see well enough ahead to know that this course, though it looked more dangerous, was equally perilous as the portside course they were on. But it would be quicker, and he had to test young Hamp's ability to answer his commands with instant obedience. Their lives, and the thin hope of their community's survival, depended upon it. "You heard me, Helm," he said. "Now!"

"Aye . . . sir," Hamp replied. He hesitated a moment longer before the king heard the familiar rolling of the wheel, the answering rudder below, and felt the slow, steady turn.

"Make all sail!" Whitson shouted.

"Make all sail!" Captain Walters echoed, and the ship's silence was shattered.

Whitson turned to see the hands aloft send the last long sails free to be tied taut by burly bucks, who fastened all secure. All three masts, the foremast near him in the front, the mainmast in the middle of the ship, and the mizzenmast far aft above the helm, were brimming with sails. The topsails high and the courses closer to the deck, every sail was set, and *Steadfast* was on the move.

Whitson felt the fast-answering speed as they raced toward the rapids.

"Shipmates!" he cried. "I know the river is perilous and we don't have enough of a crew to sail her at our best. But we have no choice." He looked back at the swift-approaching rapids, stroked his chin, then turned again to the expectant crew. "Actually, we do have a choice. We can still turn around. We can surrender." Whitson let those words roll around the deck and up to the bucks aloft in the rigging.

"Never, Your Majesty," Brindle Cove said, stepping forward beside the helm.

"Aye, never!" Jake Able cried, fist clenched.

"We can surrender our queen," Whitson said.

"Never!" Cove, Able, and all the hands aft cried. "Never!" repeated the hands in the mainmast and foremast above the king.

"We can become Grimble's pawns," Whitson continued, "and feed the vile dragons with our young."

"Never!" the whole crew shouted in unison.

"Are we *Steadfast*?" Whitson cried.

"Yes!"

"Will we surrender?"

"Never!" they all cried in return, cheering afterward with fists in the air.

"Now, bucks," Whitson called over the last of the shouts, "we must clear these rapids bravely and come through quickly so we can cut off *Desolation* in time. I need instant obedience. Trust me, and I will lead you through this. Be brave and bold."

"Aye, sir!" Lord Grant called.

"Aye, sir!" everyone shouted.

Brindle Cove leapt onto the rail before the helm. He raised a fist, then placed it over his heart. "My place beside you," he began, and they all joined in. "My blood for yours. Till the Green Ember rises, or the end of the world!"

The deck erupted in fresh ferocious cheers as Whitson bowed quickly to Brindle Cove in thanks.

Whitson turned to the impending danger. "Now, the gambit."

The ship surged ahead, and every buck stood ready at his station. Whitson scanned the route, eyes narrowed to slits. "Port one point," he cried. The answer came, but he still felt Hamp's momentary hesitation. Whitson considered alternatives, but there was no time. They had reached the rapids.

"Hold fast!" Whitson cried as they spilled into the swirling swell.

Steadfast pitched as the bow sunk down, sending foaming surges over the sides. Whitson gripped the wooden rail as he was knocked off his feet and nearly submerged in the swell. He righted himself and found his feet again as the bow rose again and the aft dipped, sending the cascade back across the deck. Several bucks tumbled back, reaching desperately for anything to arrest their slide into the deadly river. Hands reached out for sliding sailors, and many were rescued by shipmates.

Whitson wiped his face and peered into the chaos before him. A river rock twice the size of the one that had ripped *Vanguard* apart loomed just ahead. "Hard to starboard!" he cried, concerned that Hamp might not act in time.

When there was no change and the ship sped on toward the massive rock, he spun to scan the deck. The helm was there.

Vacant.

Hamp was gone.

Tales of Old Natalia

Chapter Sixteen

At sight of the dragons, all four rabbits looked at Lillie, eyes wide.

"Hide!" she whispered. They dropped to the ground and crawled to the nearby cover of a thicket pressing against the back of Galt's hovel. Once all four were inside the bramble and relatively well hidden, Galt clapped a hand over Tarn's whining mouth. Massie glanced at the queen and then risked raising his head so he could see. Soon he, the queen, and the prince were all gazing through the tangled brush at the dragons circling the pool.

There were around twenty of them, and their angry cries of a few moments before had given way to a brooding silence. They stood around the pond, their heads down, still as stone. Massie felt like his heartbeat was loud enough to be heard by every one of them. Occasionally, as a split tongue flicked out, he was certain the nearest dragons would turn and attack them.

The long silence was gradually interrupted by a slow, gurgling chant that grew in its eerie intensity. The guttural music seemed to pulse among them and shape an atmosphere that Massie felt he could almost touch, even outside their circle. A cloud passed over the sky, and the pool darkened. The chant intensified, and the dragons stomped rhythmically along with the swelling sound. A melody began among a few of the creatures, if it could be called a melody. It was a song, but it felt to Massie as though the music was all wrong. It twisted inside him, made him nauseous and confused. It was music, but music that was like food that ate its own maker. This music was wicked, and it unnerved him. The dragons stopped their stomping and waded out, chanting still, as they approached the body of their comrade in the pool. Massie looked away as the monsters leapt forward and a sound of thrashing chaos ensued.

"What do we do?" Massie asked as Queen Lillie broke away from gazing at the horrifying scene. Her eyes were wide and her mouth open.

"These are Grimble's friends?" she asked, disbelieving. "I could never have thought . . . even him ..."

"Now, Mother?" Lander asked, taking her hand. "We must get away, yes?"

"Shawhhhhhh!" the lead dragon called in a rasping command as Massie looked out to see all the creatures turn toward them. Massie froze, unable to take his eyes off the dragon master. The creature sniffed the air, his tongue flicking out, and he pointed a long-clawed finger toward them.

"Run!" Lillie cried. "Run!"

Massie sprinted into the forest, fleeing just behind the queen and the prince.

"Lead the way, Galt!" Queen Lillie cried, and the buck sped ahead toward paths known only to him. They followed hard after.

Massie glanced back at Tarn, but then quickly looked ahead again. The dragons had him. "Faster!" Massie cried, stricken with terror.

They sped on, ducking under low-hanging limbs and dodging around clusters of brush. Massie was relieved to see Lander keeping up with the swift queen, both hard on Galt's heels.

A spear sailed overhead, narrowly missing Queen Lillie. More followed, and one stuck into a wide tree just as Massie curled around it and hurried after his three companions into the thickening woods. Glancing back, Massie saw more dragons than he could easily count, and they were closer than he had hoped. Two surged ahead of their fellows, loping on all fours as they came. They made up ground with alarming speed.

Massie ran on, through forest paths and across occasional clearings. Were it not for Galt and his knowledge of the paths, Massie knew they would all be dead. He ran on, up and up, away from the pursuing monsters, fatigue screaming out for relief and rest.

At last they came to rocky ground that led to a section of caves. They passed tall, narrow trees on either side of the path, which grew sparser as they neared the rocky ridge and caves. Massie glanced back and saw that the two swiftest dragons were nearly on them. The prince looked back, and Massie was amazed to see the set of his jaw and determination in his face.

Prince Lander slowed a bit, then looked straight at Massie. "Protect the queen!" he shouted with one more backward glance at the two dragons who were nearly upon them.

Lander leapt, turning sideways and extending his hands to snag a tree, his speed whipping him around to bring his feet to meet the foremost dragon's throat in a devastating kick. Massie watched the creature buckle back, and his comrade's momentary shock provided a window of escape. Lander took it. He dashed off into an adjacent cave. The dragons pursued.

Massie sped on, shoving the disbelieving queen forward.

"Go!" Massie shouted, and Queen Lillie reluctantly ran on. Galt split through a narrow pass ahead, rock-walled on either side, and rushed on. Massie and the queen followed. They emerged onto a precipice that commanded a view of much of this side of the island. For a moment, Massie marveled at the rock-strewn foaming river below and the wide, beautiful land in every direction. Then he fell.

Massie pitched forward, falling into a tumbling roll as he and the queen careened down the mountainside behind Galt's more elegant sliding descent.

Above them, the angry, gurgling roar of the dragons filled the air.

Chapter Seventeen

Whitson's eyes widened as he sprinted for the vacant helm. Hamp had disappeared, and the entire aft of the ship was a sloshing chaotic jumble. Glancing back at the ship-splitting rock looming just ahead, he saw that he would never make it to the wheel in time. He braced for the impact but saw a dark, lithe form slide down a mizzenmast sail and drop down onto the deck, wrenching the wheel hard over as he landed.

Brindle Cove!

Whitson nearly leapt for joy at the sight of the red rabbit at the wheel. He turned, wincing as *Steadfast* narrowly slipped alongside the colossal rock. The crew, those who were aware enough to see it, gave a shout. Brindle Cove had taken the

117

helm. He was the helmer, now.

"Helmer, there!" King Whitson shouted, and Lieutenant Cove saluted his king.

The crew shouted, "Helmer!" and cheered him as they recovered their stations, coiling rope and standing ready at the sails.

"Take in the topsails!" Whitson cried, noting the incredible pace at which they sailed. The wind had picked up again. "Courses only, if you please, Captain Walters."

"Aye, sir," Walters answered. "Take in topsails!" he repeated loudly while helping to dislodge Jimmi Docker from a tangle of rope.

Whitson spun and scanned the rapids, spotting two rocks they were likely to hit if they turned hard either way. "Lieutenant Cove!" he cried. "One point starboard, then hold her steady!"

"Aye, sir!" Brindle Cove answered as a surge of fresh rapids sprayed over him. He tilted the wheel, then held it firmly and set his feet.

"Steady!" Whitson called, eyes ahead at the rocks and hand extended aft toward the helm. "Steady!" He spotted a steep drop dead ahead, just past the two rocks. Whitson scanned the surrounding river. "On my mark, Helmer, bring her hard to port!"

"Aye, sir. Ready!" Brindle Cove said, gritting his teeth and squinting against the spray.

"Steady!" Whitson called as *Steadfast* slipped between the two rocks with a mere hand's width of margin on either side. "Steady!" the king repeated amid the gasping crew, waving his hand slowly up and down as he gazed fixedly ahead. "Now, Lieutenant!" he called, pointing aft.

Brindle Cove swung the wheel hard over, sending *Steadfast* lurching left toward the island's rocky bank at an alarming pace. On shore, a stone outcropping lay ahead, a high craggy cliff that might snap the mainmast if they got too close.

"Starboard now, Helmer!" Whitson shouted. "A few points, then ease back. And loose topsails!"

"Loose topsails!" Walters cried, and the hands aloft let fly the sails, then fixed them firm. The sails billowed out, catching the wind as the turn came, speeding *Steadfast* along the shoreline and around the swirling drop that roiled and foamed in the middle of the river. It had been the only way around the watery maw, but the shallow depth along the riverbank shoal and the rocky outcropping threatened to make them suffer for their narrow escape.

"Helmer, there!" Whitson cried. "Do you see it?"

"Aye, sir," Brindle Cove called. "I see it."

"Get us around it, Lieutenant," Whitson said, eyeing the clifftop warily, "without dropping us into that churning deathtrap hard to starboard."

"Aye, sir!"

Just then, they saw three forms sprinting along the jutting rock. Whitson cried out, "Lillie? *Lillie*!" It *was* his wife! With her was Lieutenant Massie and another rabbit—*Galt! So the old traitor returned to help after all.* His heart sank not to see his son, but he had no time to indulge in despair. They were running for their lives. "Take in sail!" Whitson cried, grunting as he grasped a handhold and propelled himself further up the rigging. Walters repeated the order. The hands worked quickly to obey the king. "Get us closer, Lieutenant Cove!"

"Aye, sir!" Cove called, easing the nimble ship closer to the dangerous jutting rock. The outcropping narrowed at the edge and looked unstable, with small loose rocks already breaking off as the three fleeing rabbits pounded along it.

King Whitson leapt for the rigging and clambered up the foremast to the main yard. "Drop anchor!" he shouted as he edged along the sturdy beam, dodging busy shipmates and darting glances at the three escaping rabbits. For they were fleeing, that was clear. "Closer, Helmer!" he shouted.

"Aye, sir," Cove replied, wincing as he nudged the wheel, the ship edging delicately closer. The king hurried on, balancing as he rushed high aloft amid the ship's swaying sails and frantic crew.

The rabbits ashore ran on as large monsters—the wicked dragons Galt had described—appeared behind them and rushed toward the fleeing three.

Some bore spears, and all looked capable of the worst horrors should they reach their prey.

"Jump!" Whitson cried as Galt's haunted face appeared on the brittle ledge. Galt did leap, catching the outstretched hand of a strong sailor, who pulled him to safety. Next Lillie leapt, landing nimbly on the main yard and tumbling into Whitson's arms, nearly knocking them out of the ship's heights. Whitson's heart swelled as he gathered her close, and eager bucks all around made certain they were secure.

Massie followed last, leaping from the precipice with a desperate bound. The foremast was moving past, and he missed his grip, slipping onto the bundled foretopsail. The vast cloth unfurled with him as he tumbled down. He seemed certain to end by smashing onto the deck far below, but he snagged a dangling rope and swung awkwardly to roll on the deck as the ship slowed somewhat with the drag of the anchor. But they were going too fast for the anchor rope to hold. It checked their frantic pace a moment, then bent the ship sideways before snapping as *Steadfast* leapt forward again.

"Archers!" Captain Walters cried. "Fire!" The

industrious captain had gathered the archers while the king ran aloft, and now the seven bucks sent their shafts at those dragons poised on the cliff's edge. Most of the arrows didn't penetrate the rough armor-like scales of the beasts, but two of them fell, wounded, when arrows found their exposed bellies. The dragons sent whizzing spears at the archers. Two rabbits fell to the deck.

Whitson and Lillie descended as the remaining archers sent their desperate volleys. The foremast had drifted past the precipice with only inches to spare, and the mainmast, the large central beam amidships, was nearing the dragons on the point.

Whitson landed on deck, then spun to see the five dragons looming above on the cliff's edge.

And there was Lander, his only son, racing away from ten more dragons behind him and straight toward the five monsters ahead of him at the end of the cliff.

"No!" Whitson cried.

Tales of Old Natalia

Chapter Eighteen

Lillie saw it all. Exhausted from her narrow escape and weak from hunger, she looked up at her son, running for his life.

"Lander!" Whitson shouted, springing aloft once more. He rushed up the foremast and across the rigging, toward the mainmast, which was now near enough to strike the cliff's top edge.

At the same time, Lieutenant Cove steered the ship hard to port, moving the mainmast even closer to the cliff.

Lieutenant Massie retrieved a bow from a fallen archer and accepted an arrow offered by another. He closed one eye, nocked the arrow, and drew.

Lander dashed down the cliff, barely out of reach of the foremost monster behind him and nearly to the five dragons that waited at the end of the cliff. Massie let loose the arrow, which sped between Lander's ears and into the heart of the grasping dragon behind him. He fell, rolling at the feet of the dragons in pursuit, tripping them up for a moment.

Cove's course correction sent the mainmast slamming into the cliff's edge. Lillie expected the tall beam to buckle and break off, sending the sails to the deck. But the mainmast held, somehow, and broke free the loose rocks on the cliff's edge. The edge of the precipice crumbled and fell, taking the five dragons down in a hail of falling rock. The pilot's quick correction sent the ship back toward the river's middle, escaping most of the plunging stone, but not all. Two of the dragons fell clattering to the deck.

Lillie cried out as Lander leapt from the crumbling cliff and snagged the outstretched hand of a swinging Jake Able, whose mates held him fast while he dangled high above the topsails of the mizzenmast.

"I'll not drop you, Your Highness!" Jake cried. "And they'll not drop me," he added, glancing back at his shipmates deliberately.

One of the dragons on deck lay still, but the other leapt up, bellowing a coarse challenge and baring his awful teeth. The first sailor reached him from behind and sent a sword slice down the beast's back. The sword snapped in half, and the dragon glanced over his shoulder, his tail whipping back to thrash the sailor. The dragon's tail struck the buck with such force that he smashed through the rail and plunged, lifeless, into the river. The crew fell back, and Lillie, frozen on deck, stood before the monster. He charged. She snapped out of her daze, but it was too late. The beast was upon her.

Then a blur of fur blinded Lillie, and she was knocked back, rolling on the deck. When she looked up again, Galt stood over the dragon.

The dead dragon.

"Protect the queen," Galt said, nodding to the prince.

Lillie rose slowly as Lander and Whitson rushed to embrace her.

Tales of Old Natalia

Chapter Nineteen

After a short time, in which Whitson heard a hurried account of Lillie's and Lander's ordeals, Captain Walters recalled Whitson to his duty. "Your Majesty, the rapids."

Whitson recovered himself, said, "Thank you, Captain," and hurried to the bow. His keen eyes took in the last of the roiling drop behind and to their left, and then he internalized the scene spreading out ahead of them downriver. "Three points to starboard, if you please, Lieutenant Cove," he said, resuming his place in the bow.

"Aye, Your Majesty," Cove answered. The ship eased right, creaking as it came about.

Whitson turned to survey the mainmast. "Topsails, if you please, Captain Walters. But only at the fore and mizzen."

"Topsails, fore and mizzenmasts only," Walters cried out, and the crew resumed their work. Many toiled at making the best of the damage on deck from the falling rocks, which Whitson believed was minor. If only the mainmast's damage were minimal. He would receive damage and casualty reports soon. He hated hearing the casualties.

Ships can be mended. Not so, the fallen.

But his family was here—somehow, here—and his heart soared at the knowledge.

Steadfast skirted a dangerous section of the river by crossing to the opposite side and then continued to navigate the passage through lesser perils for a period. Whitson glanced back amidships at Lillie. She gave him a weary smile and then led Lander below. Galt followed.

Massie, looking haggard, approached the bow.

"Let me guess," Whitson said to Captain Walters. "Lieutenant Massie refused to take rest and begged to be allowed to return to duty?"

"Aye, sir," Walters said, smiling wryly.

"Perhaps," Whitson said, looking at Massie, "you will respond to the order of one a little above the rank of captain?"

Massie bowed. "I am Your Majesty's servant," he said, keeping his head down, "and I want to help."

"You may help me by doing what you have been doing, *Captain* Massie."

Massie looked up. "Your Majesty?"

"Yes, Captain. I am promoting you this day and this moment ordering you to go below and see to my family. Eat and drink with them. Get a little rest, if you can."

"But sir—" Massie began.

"No, Massie," Whitson said, glancing back at the river. "No more argument." To the helm, the king said, "Port, two points, if you please."

"Aye, sir," came Cove's answer.

Whitson returned his attention to Massie. Massie bowed again and turned to head toward the hatch.

"One more thing, Captain," Whitson said. "While you recover, think about this. What will we do if—*when*—we reach *Desolation*? Captain Grimble has a heavier, stronger, better-equipped ship. He has more than twice our crew and triple our weaponry. He knows these waters, and we don't. He is an excellent sailor and has allies in these creatures," he motioned to the dragon being tossed overboard. "I have a small, tired crew. I have a creaking mainmast that could go at any moment. We sail into unknown waters. He has every advantage, Massie, and I *must* beat him."

"You have us," Lord Grant said, easing up beside the king and motioning all around to the small but eager crew. "It's not you and him. It's us and them. We are with you, poor and tired—and old—as we may be, to the very end."

"Till the end of the world," Massie said, fist over his heart.

Tales of Old Natalia

Chapter Twenty

Massie stood on deck, peering into the distance as the sun dipped lower. It was early evening, and he had rested a little as the king commanded. He had eaten with the queen, the prince, and Galt. They all stood on deck now. As Jerin Carpenter led a team binding the mainmast around with their best new rope, the king held a council just aft of the foremast, between Massie at the bow and Jerin's team.

"Bring them here," Captain Walters said, and Massie looked over his shoulder to see Frill Able and Baily Nocks bringing up blastpowder barrels. Walters nodded, and the two broke the seals.

The king looked inside. "Aye," he said.

Walters nodded again, and the hands carried

the large barrels back toward the hatch. Massie frowned, resuming his survey of the river ahead. The rapids had grown tamer since he had been on deck, though he had been below during a turbulent section that seemed to go on and on and which they were all glad to have survived.

"Will it do?" Lord Grant asked.

"It will. So that is our plan," King Whitson said, concluding the council. "We go, shipmates. It might mean death. But we must go."

"Be assured, sir," Brindle Cove said, "if you go to die, then we die with you."

"To the very end, sir," Massie said, turning to add his voice.

"To the end, sir," the rest said in a stuttering chorus.

Looking forward again, Massie wiped at his eyes. He felt that the promise held a dread. He couldn't say why, but he felt an inner certainty that he would not see the next day's sunrise. He tried to shake off the feeling, but it persisted.

It is either war or surrender. And we cannot surrender. It's a cause worth dying for.

Massie saw what he thought might be the edge of the island. There was movement on the bank. "Your Majesty, if you please?" he called.

"What is it, Captain?" Whitson asked, jogging up.

Massie pointed to the shapes in the distance and the widening water that meant the end of the island and the rejoining of the two sections of the river.

"Helmer, there!" the king called. "Hard to starboard."

"Aye, sir," Brindle Cove answered. "Hard to starboard it is." The ship answered, and *Steadfast* bent her course right.

"Take us near the far bank, but watch out for the shoals."

"Aye, sir," Brindle answered.

"Archers, at the ready," Whitson called.

"Archers, ready!" Captain Walters repeated.

Massie bowed to the king and then ran to join the archers. He had inherited a quiver and bow from a fallen shipmate.

"Captain, if you please?" Jerin Carpenter said, a knuckle to his forehead in front of Captain Walters.

"Yes, Master Carpenter?" Walters replied.

"Sir, we might set the square sail on the mainmast," Jerin said, motioning at the rope-bound mast, "but I wouldn't trust her with topsails except at the direst need."

"Thank you, sir," Walters said, and Jerin moved aft to see to a broken rail.

Captain Walters looked to the king, who had heard the exchange, a question in his expression.

"We will set the square sail only at the main, if you please, Captain Walters," Whitson said, peering at the shapes on the shore.

"Set main course!" Captain Walters cried, and he was instantly obeyed.

Massie looked past the peering king at the forms on shore. There was something familiar about them.

"Captain Massie, there," King Whitson said, motioning for Massie to rejoin him at the bow. Massie scampered up, sliding in place between the king and Captain Walters.

"Is it?" King Whitson began.

"Could it be?" Captain Walters asked.

"Aye, sir," Massie said, smiling wide. "It's our own. Survivors of the wreck, to be sure!"

"There's my Rose!" Jake Able called out. "I thought she was lost!"

More of the crew saw loved ones on shore,

and Massie wept as he spotted dear friends of his own. Standing at the head of the rabbits waving on shore was Mother Saramack herself.

"This changes things," King Whitson said. "Helmer, hard to port! Take in sail."

"Aye, sir. Hard to port!' Cove replied.

"Take in sail!" Walters cried. The hands hurried to bring in the sails.

"Captain Walters, who is our best swimmer?" Whitson asked.

"I am." Queen Lillie stepped forward, a bow strung over her shoulder. "And I think I know what you're thinking."

The royal family had a hurried conference, and then Queen Lillie and Prince Lander disappeared below, along with Jake Able.

"Massie, take the bow lookout," Whitson ordered, and Massie saluted. Then the king hurried back to the helm, where he gathered the leaders of each of the ship's sections. Captain Walters listened intently, then broke off and climbed up to issue orders to bucks aloft in the rigging. The king's hurried council continued, and Massie glanced back to see Frill Able nodding, a toothless grin breaking out at the king's intense instruction. Jerin Carpenter frowned, casting an anxious glance at his battered mainmast, then nodded to the king.

Massie looked forward again at the river ahead, smoother now as they neared the junction of the two sections. He gazed at the shore, delighted to see so many faces that were feared to have perished. Then his smile disappeared. "There!" he called, pointing over the heads of the rabbits stranded on the island.

It was *Desolation* emerging from the river beyond.

Chapter Twenty-One

B attle stations!" Whitson cried, as *Steadfast* continued its course to bring it alongside the stranded rabbits on shore. The king ran forward and embraced Lander, then looked into Lillie's eyes. "You know what to do?"

"Aye. I do," she said, winking at him. He kissed her and then watched as she and Lander dove into the water and swam for the shore. A few others followed, including Jake Able, with a rope tied to his waist that extended to a barrel bobbing behind him as he swam.

Desolation emerged into the wide river at the edge of the island as *Steadfast* shot ahead.

"Four points to starboard, Helmer!"

"Aye, sir!"

"Make all sail, if you please, Captain Walters."

"Make all sail!" Walters called.

The sails were sheeted home poorly, and it took far longer than it should have. The main foretopsail was half spilled and flapped in the wind. The mizzen course was flapping too, and the angry shouts of officers harried hapless sailors, who failed again and again to secure that sail.

Whitson glanced back at *Desolation*. She was making all sail and giving chase.

"She's gaining!" he cried, shouting as loud as he could at his inept crew. "Get that sail secure, you lubbers!"

The officers berated the crew, and Brindle Cove jerked the wheel, spilling the wind and sending *Steadfast* peeling back toward *Desolation*.

"Cove, you fool!" Whitson cried.

"Beg pardon, sir!" Cove shouted, regaining the correct course. But it had cost *Steadfast* dearly. *Desolation* was gaining more and more. Triumphant shouts carried across the water as Grimble's crew watched the distance between them and their chase shorten.

"Secure that sail, Frill Able!" Captain Walters cried, fist shaking at the clumsy crew working the mainsails. Just then Baily Nocks fell from the main yard to land awkwardly on deck. Several bucks gathered around to help Nocks, including Brindle Cove, and *Steadfast* careened off to starboard, spilling wind once again and turning toward the shore of the mainland.

Whitson screamed with a rage no one had ever heard before. "Back to your stations!" He drew his sword and drove the hands away from the sailor splayed out on deck. "Leave him! Cove, to the helm!"

Whitson could feel Grimble's gaze and hear the exultant cries and snickering laughter of *Desolation*'s crew. Cove regained the wheel and continued the turn so that *Steadfast* was headed back to the island. Whitson heard Grimble's eager commands as *Desolation* turned in a neat maneuver, closing the distance between the two ships with expert ease. The massive ship loomed large, closer and closer, and the *Steadfast*'s crew began to panic. They faltered, freezing at their duties in full view of the keen *Desolations*. Grimble's bucks were armed to the teeth, fairly overflowing the rails with eagerness to board and take *Steadfast*. The sheer number of them was daunting. Steel flashed, officers shouted commands, and their well-armed party seemed certain to crush *Steadfast*'s hapless crew if they could only close the short distance between the two ships.

Whitson raged on the chaotic deck of *Steadfast*. "Back to your stations!" he cried again, rushing through the commotion at the bow to disappear behind a wall of flapping sail that Captain Walters and Captain Suttfin were trying to bring up for the mainmast. Whitson grabbed the axe laid by the mainmast and swung it hard at the ropes binding the fractured mast. The ropes snapped free, and the tall tree of a mast groaned. Whitson swung the axe again and again, chopping away at the creaking mast itself. He sprinted back to the bow and waded into the muddled crew there, sending them scattering with his sword.

"They're right on top of us, sir!" Walters cried. Whitson spun to see *Desolation* looming large just aft and starboard of the struggling *Steadfast*. He saw Grimble's proud expression, the eager faces of the bucks around him. For the first time, he saw the ruby gem around Grimble's neck. Captain Grimble had taken the Ruling Stone.

He raised his voice again, but it sounded different now. "Make all sail, if you please, Captain Walters," he said, smiling. His voice was loud, but it had regained its confidence and ease of command.

"Make all sail, if you please!" Walters repeated, his voice also resuming its usual calm.

The effect was instant. The flapping sails were sheeted home at once, and Brindle Cove slipped the swift ship into the perfect course to maximize the wind, now filling every sail. The mainmast creaked, but *Steadfast* surged ahead, widening the thin gap between her and *Desolation*.

Whitson heard the curses from Captain Grimble and his crew, then Grimble's cry of "Archers, to the rails!"

"Lieutenant Cove, if you please," Whitson said, nodding to the helm. "On my mark."

"Aye, sir," Cove replied, eager eyes on his king.

Whitson looked ahead at the island, then back over at *Desolation*. He breathed deep, gauging every distance. After a few more agonizing seconds, he pointed at Cove. "Mark! Port, now!"

Brindle Cove cranked the wheel, sending *Steadfast* on a jarring leftward course. The crew held tight as the ship leaned hard with the sudden turn. But just as soon as the turn left came and they seemed to spurt away from *Desolation*, Whitson shouted once more.

"Hard to starboard, Helmer!"

Brindle Cove was ready. The whole ship was ready, despite the pretended panic and poor sailing they had played for show during the chase. Each held fast as the pilot pitched the ship back to starboard in a dazzling reversal that nearly turned the ship over.

But the ship did not turn over. The course correction sent her sailing, with incredible speed, straight at *Desolation*.

Captain Grimble's panicked commands to turn were too late. *Steadfast*'s bow crashed into *Desolation*'s middle, tearing deep into the massive ship. The mainmast on *Steadfast* snapped, and it fell in a hail of rope and sails onto Grimble's deck.

Chapter Twenty-Two

Massie was perched high on the mizzenmast when *Steadfast* ripped into *Desolation*. He held on with all his might as the speeding ship grinded to a halt amidships of the bigger vessel. He watched from his secret perch as the mainmast and mainsails came down and Grimble's deck was thrown into panic.

They were stunned. Massie reveled in the confusion caused by the king's bold maneuver. But it didn't last. Grimble was no fool. He still had the overwhelming advantage, and he regained control of his crew quickly.

Captain Grimble reorganized his boarders, bucks now more furious and desperate to destroy *Steadfast*'s smaller, vulnerable crew. They cut through the mainmast sails and surged onto the deck of *Steadfast*, angry curses and hate-filled threats accompanying the streaming pack of indignant, well-armed warriors.

They poured onto *Steadfast*'s deck but, to their great surprise, found no one there. The deck was clear of sailors and almost entirely clear of anything at all. Massie watched with a curling smile as they stomped around, then ran to the rails, assuming that *Steadfast*'s crew had all abandoned ship.

Then a shocked cry rang out from the most advanced boarder, who had now reached far aft on *Steadfast*. "Captain Grimble!" he cried. "Abandon ship!"

All eyes on deck turned to the corner, where ten large barrels were fitted with rags. The rags were burning against the edge of the barrels.

"Blastpowder barrels!" another boarder cried, and he leapt into the water. Massie peered down at the sudden panic on deck as *Desolation*'s boarders, determined with a violent hunger moments before, now fled *Steadfast*'s deck in a wild frenzy. Most of the bucks leapt from the deck and landed in the river, swimming for the shore. Some fled back to *Desolation*. Massie watched as Captain

Grimble ran for the rail, then paused and gazed at the barrels. The Ruling Stone swung beneath his chin as he paused.

His face curled in disgust as he ran to the barrels and kicked the first one over. It burst open to reveal—nothing. "I know him. I knew he couldn't—" He broke open each in turn and found the barrels all empty. "Whitson!" he raged, calling his remaining crew back.

But the last of his bucks were not the only ones to surge back on deck. King Whitson, as if called out by Grimble's loud challenge, burst through the hatch and led his bucks back onto *Steadfast*'s deck. Defiant shouts poured from the brave crew as they met the reduced but still fierce foes from the enemy ship.

Massie saw the forms of Grimble's fleeing crew swimming toward the island as the remainder fought on deck. Now the numbers were closer to even. As Whitson broke through a press of enemies and fought his way to Captain Grimble, Massie set to work with his bow, felling the reinforcements that threatened to join the fight from *Desolation*. He pinned them back as long as he could before swinging down and joining the fight.

Massie shouldered his bow and ripped free his sword as he waded into the wild battle on deck. He blocked a strike from a massive buck, then bent to sweep the bigger foe's feet with a spinning kick. Another enemy leapt at him, sword flashing past his head. Massie sidestepped the attacker and brought his own sword around to slash his opponent.

The bloody battle raged on, and Massie got lost in the close, chaotic rhythm of the contest. He felt that the king's side was gaining the upper hand when a strike from behind, half-deflected by a lunging block from Baily Nocks, caught him on the shoulder. Massie pitched forward, dropping his sword as he reached to cover the wound. He rolled on the deck, on fire from the pain and dazed by his rough tumble.

When he got to his knees, he shook his head. He rose slowly, gazing all around. He saw the king in the distance, locked in brutal battle with Captain Grimble. Grimble seemed to have the better of the exchanges Massie saw, and his heart sank as he remembered the reputation for sword skill the traitor Grimble possessed.

Then Massie saw him. One buck of Grimble's cursed crew had gotten behind the king. Grimble drove Whitson back as the assassin surged up behind the king, blade bared.

Chapter Twenty-Three

From her concealed position on the island, Lillie peered out over the pebbly river shore, eyes searching for Whitson among the bucks battling on deck.

"They're coming, Mother," Lander said, hand on his sword hilt. She looked from her son to the river again, where Grimble's crew was coming ashore in large numbers. These were those who had fallen for Whitson's ruse and abandoned ship in a mad dash. Now they stumbled onto land, angry as they looked back at the ship—the unexploded ship—and their comrades fighting a desperate battle.

Commander Usher, Captain Grimble's most loyal confederate, was gathering a group to swim back out to the ships and overwhelm the king.

"Don't move," Queen Lillie said, walking out from the brush and over the small ridge that rose between the forest and the shore. "Lay down your arms, and surrender."

Commander Usher looked back at her, puzzled for a moment, then broke into laughter. His bucks, more and more coming ashore each moment, joined in. "I am glad to see you, Queen," he said. "It looks like our comrades may have . . . misplaced you." He nodded to a burly buck nearby. "Orban will remain with you until we come back." He turned back to the water. "To the fight!" he cried as Orban swaggered toward the queen with a smirk on his face.

An arrow sped over Usher's head and splashed in the river. He spun around to see the ridge lined with unusual archers. Twenty stood firm, arrows nocked. Jake Able and Jones Brine were the only bucks among them. The rest were does. Many of them were among the older widows, including Mother Saramack, king's councilor.

Lander stood beside the queen, his face determined and his sword pointed at Orban.

Commander Usher looked alarmed for a

moment, then smiled. "A bunch of does and old crones. You don't have the guts to—" he began, stepping forward. But an arrow swished through the air, and Usher spun down with a groan.

Mother Saramack stepped forward, nocking another arrow. "You left defenseless children to die, bargained us all away to dragons," she said, almost spitting with anger. "You think we don't have the resolve to fight you? It's a mercy we don't end you all right now. Make another move forward, and you'll find out how ready we are to do what we must."

The bucks looked at one another, bewildered and, Lillie thought, a little ashamed. Ashamed of what, she wasn't sure.

"Your weapons," Lillie said, all competence and command. "Cast them down." Slowly, the bucks began throwing down their swords. "To your knees," she continued. They knelt.

While her makeshift militia, overseen by Mother Saramack, saw to the prisoners, she ascended the ridge once more and gazed out at the battle on board *Steadfast*. She looked for Whitson amid the fray.

When she found him and saw his outline set clear against the dipping sun, she cried out, "No!"

Tales of Old Natalia

Chapter Twenty-Four

Massie's eyes widened as King Whitson was driven back by Captain Grimble's expert sword attack and another enemy surged in behind, dagger poised to kill the king. Massie leapt up, reaching back with his left hand for an arrow from his quiver while his right hand pulled his bow from his shoulder. He winced in agony as his wound flared painfully, but his motion never stopped. Ignoring the pain, and the battle all around him, Massie focused everything he had on his target. He had to kill that attacker before he got to the king. The bow came level as he nocked and loosed the arrow in a desperate half-balanced shot.

Massie feared that he had missed.

"No!" he shouted, wincing at the agonizing pain rippling through his shoulder and, worse, the terrible scene he watched as his arrow sped away.

The attacker raised his blade back farther than Massie had expected. The arrow caught his hand!

* * *

Whitson was running out of strength. Captain Grimble seemed invincible with a sword, and Whitson fought against a rising certainty that he could never defeat him. Grimble's hard strike and quick shuffle sideways sent Whitson pitching back. He could tell Grimble was forcing him back, but he couldn't stop it or sneak a glance behind himself. It was all he could do to fend off Grimble's relentless and skillful assault.

Then he heard the swish of an arrow and a scream from behind. Whitson spun and struck down the attacker behind him in a powerful twisting strike.

Continuing his spin, he brought his blade around with enough force to split Grimble in two. But Captain Grimble, though shocked at Whitson's eluding his trap, was aware enough to bring his blade quickly around to block Whitson's devastating stroke.

Now Grimble, seizing the advantage, drove his blade down at the king. Whitson dodged, and Grimble's sword sliced through the aft railing. Whitson stabbed at Grimble, but he stepped aside and brought his own blade back in a deft slash that caught Whitson's leg. Pain screamed for attention, but Whitson limped to his feet, sword up in defense as he grimaced in pain.

"It's over, Whitson," Grimble said, cackling.

"No," the king replied.

"No?"

"You took my wife and stole the Ruling Stone," Whitson said, sending a swipe at Grimble's head. Grimble blocked the stroke and stepped back. "You left half the community to be killed!" Another strike. Grimble blocked again and took a few more steps back. "You traded us away to dragons!" Whitson shouted, bringing his blade around in a desperate overhead strike. Grimble blocked it easily and kicked Whitson back. The king fell hard, striking his head on deck. Dazed, he got to his knees slowly.

"Give up, Whitson," Grimble cried, fingering the ruby around his neck. "I will be a new king for a new time. You know you can't defeat me!"

Whitson saw a blurred outline, then three forms slowly merging into one as he blinked away his confusion and his eyes finally focused on Grimble's. He rose slowly, stepping forward for a final, fatal attack. Then he stopped, shook his head, and looked around.

Massie was there, bow poised. Brindle Cove was there, blade in hand and breathing hard. Jimmi Docker was there, oar in hand like a club. Baily Nocks, Captains Walters and Suttfin, Frill Able, and Lord Grant were all there. Galt was there. He looked past them to the others, who held the last of Grimble's crew captive.

They had won. His Steadfasts had overcome the Desolations.

"You can never defeat me, Whitson!" Grimble repeated, enraged and desperate.

"I don't have to," Whitson said, motioning to his bucks gathered around him. "They already have."

Grimble's eyes grew wild with desperation. He lunged forward, rushing the king with his sword. Jimmi Docker stepped forward and spun, swinging his oar in an expert arc that collided, crunching, with Grimble's face.

The renegade captain crumbled in a heap.

Whitson bent and snatched the ruby medallion, breaking the chain that hung around Grimble's neck.

Chapter Twenty-Five

Whitson found Lillie and Lander on shore, and he ran to embrace them. Captains Walters and Suttfin saw to the prisoners. Lord Grant and Captain Massie led the provisioning for the loyal rabbits on both sides of the island.

They had not lost so many as he had feared. The good reports encouraged Whitson and helped him press on through deep exhaustion.

"You must rest, Whitson," Lillie said, taking a dry blanket from a line before passing it on to Lander, who folded it and added it to a growing stack. The Green Ember dangled from the prince's neck.

"We all need sleep, and we will get some soon," Whitson replied, looking over at a group of children whose parents had not yet been located. "But first we must see them settled."

Lillie nodded, took up the stack of blankets, and carried them. Whitson watched her a moment, then took a box of provisions from an approaching buck and walked over as well. Lander followed, and together they made sure each child had something to eat and drink.

"It's the king himself," a young doe whispered, tears in her eyes. "Thank you, Your Majesty."

"We'll get through this," Whitson said, "together. We'll never abandon you."

Mother Saramack approached, bowing to the king and queen.

"Mother," King Whitson said, taking her hands, "thank you."

"Your Majesty is kind," she replied, "but I did only what any loyal subject would have."

"No one can do what you do," Lillie said, hugging the old widow.

"Your Majesty," Saramack said, her face turning serious. "A survivor came from Lord Grimble's company. He had been at the intended rendezvous Lord Grimble had planned with the dragons at their sacred pool."

"A survivor?" Whitson asked.

"Aye, sir," she answered. "The dragons were not pleased that Lord Grimble had been unable to secure what was promised, and they blamed him for what happened at the pool." Lillie glanced at Lander.

"The dragons—" Whitson began.

"They left only this one alive," she said, "and they sent a message by him."

"What message?" Lander asked.

"That they go to report to their king what has happened here. That they will return and finish what was intended."

"How long do we have, I wonder?" Whitson asked.

"Galt believes we might have several months," Saramack said, gripping the bow she still had around her shoulder. "But it can't be long, sire."

"Thank you, Mother," Whitson said. Then, looking gravely at his son, he said, "We have more work to do, it seems, before we reach our home."

"We have lost so much in the wreck," Lillie said, tears in her eyes. "We will have to rebuild . . . again."

"I am afraid to think of all we lost," Whitson said, sitting heavily. "The souls, added to the others lost since we left Golden Coast, will weigh heavy on my mind. But more. We have lost important things. Practical things, yes, but also things that tied us to our past. Sacred things."

"Your Majesties," Mother Saramack said, "I did find a crate on the shore near here. It's where I came to land after the wreck."

"That's good," Lillie said, trying to sound cheerful.

"It had King Gerrard's seal on it," Mother Saramack said.

Whitson's eyes brightened, and he exchanged hopeful glances with Lillie. "Where, Mother?"

She led them to the place. The battered crate with the old king's sign lay amid more wreckage of *Vanguard* strewn down the riverbank.

"I wasn't the only ancient thing to wash up here," Mother Saramack said.

They smiled, then fell silent as they walked closer.

"Could it be?" Lillie whispered as Whitson approached the crate and bent down. He touched his ears, his eyes, then his mouth, and then began breaking open the seal.

Lander stood behind his father, watching over his shoulder as the crate came open. "What is that?" he whispered, pointing inside. "Is that it? Is that *the* sword?"

"Yes, son," Whitson said. "That is Flint's stone sword itself. Some say it fell from the stars, from the warrior's cluster."

"I hope the star sword didn't break in the wreck," Lander said.

"Do you know what Fay's book says about Flint's sword, son?" Lillie asked, bending beside them to peer into the open crate of old treasures.

"No," he whispered.

Lillie touched her ears, eyes, then her mouth and went on. "'It will never break,' Fay said, 'until all the breaking is broken.'"

"Until all the breaking is broken," Lander repeated, his voice thick with reverence.

"And more than that," Mother Saramack added. "About the sword, Fay said that 'When the Mending comes, it will be unmendable.'"

"Does that mean the wars will all be over forever?" Lander asked.

"I think so, son," Lillie said.

"Is it broken, Father?" Lander asked, longing etched into every feature of his expression. He looked older than he should have.

Whitson sighed, then looked back into the crate and reached for the sword. It shone black against the pale wood of the crate. He gripped the hilt and lifted it out. It was light and felt right in his hands. More than right. It felt almost a part of him. It was a lovely blade, believed to have been forged by Flint himself from the sky stone. It was a marvel, one he almost felt unworthy to touch.

And it was whole.

Unbroken.

"I'm afraid we have more wars to fight, son." Whitson sighed, laying the blade back in the crate. "I'm very sorry for that."

"We must do our part," Lander said, eyes shining, "till the old blade is broken."

"Till the ancient blade is broken," Mother Saramack echoed.

The End

ABOUT THE AUTHOR

S. D. Smith is the author of *The Green Ember Series,* a middle-grade adventure saga. Smith's books are captivating readers across the world who are hungry for "new stories with an old soul." Enthusiastic families can't get enough of these tales.

Vintage adventure. Moral imagination. Classic virtue. Finally, stories we all love. Just one more chapter, please!

When he's not writing adventurous tales of #Rabbits WithSwords in his writing shed, dubbed The Forge, Smith loves to speak to audiences about storytelling, creation, and seeing yourself as a character in The Story.

S. D. Smith lives in West Virginia with his wife and four kids.

www.sdsmith.net

ABOUT THE ILLUSTRATOR

In seventh grade, a kid sitting behind Zach Franzen in music class reached into a ziplock bag of pencil bits and hurled some pieces at his head. Zach whipped around and threw his pen at the assailant. It turned once in the air and stuck in the boy's forehead. This is a true story. An onlooker, desiring to confirm what he witnessed, repeated, "It stuck in his head." These days Zach seeks to use his pen, pencil, or brush to create images. Hopefully, these images might have force enough to stick in the heads of those who see them.

Zach lives in North Carolina with his wife and their daughters. The Franzens love to drink tea, read stories, sing harmonies, perform in plays, paint, eat (but not eat paint), and take walks.

www.zachfranzen.com

FREE
AUDIOBOOK

sdsmith.net/freeaudio

FOLLOW SAM
ON INSTAGRAM

WANT TO BE FIRST TO GET NEWS ON NEW *GREEN EMBER* BOOKS, S. D. SMITH AUTHOR EVENTS, AND MORE?

Join S. D. Smith's newsletter.
www.sdsmith.net/updates

No spam, just Sam. Sam Smith. Author.
Dad. Eater of cookies.

Green Ember illustrator Zach Franzen
created these beautiful coloring pages.

HELMER

PICKET

HEATHER

When you give S. D. Smith five, they are free for you
to download as thanks for your support.

www.sdsmith.net/gimme5